'The first [story] is a poignant, moving portrait of human endurance; the second, a cleverly crafted exercise in suspense . . . Messud is an expert storyteller. Her style is precise and illuminating, transforming the mundane into the unusual . . . dazzling' *Observer*

'Messud proves to be as much an accomplished storyteller as an immaculate stylist . . . She is a mistress of parenthesis, the telling aside, the unspoken . . . With the short novel, Claire Messud, like Alice Munro, has found her ideal form' *Daily Telegraph*

'Two short novels of remarkable power and artistry' *Financial Times*

'[The language] speaks with both precision and beauty . . . illuminating' *Guardian*

'Superb . . . Messud's ability to filter her rich imagination through brilliantly precise prose allows her to show the kernel of redemption in even the most unlikely of human alliances' *Sunday Times*

The Hunters

Claire Messud was born in the United States in 1966. She was educated at Yale and Cambridge. Her first novel, *When the World was Steady*, was a finalist for the PEN/ Faulkner Award 1996. Her second novel, *The Last Life*, won the Encore Prize. She lives in Washington.

Claire Messud
The Hunters

TWO SHORT NOVELS

PICADOR

First published 2001 by Harcourt, Inc., New York

First published in Great Britain 2002 by Picador

This paperback edition published 2003 by Picador
an imprint of Pan Macmillan Ltd
Pan Macmillan, 20 New Wharf Road, London N1 9RR
Basingstoke and Oxford
Associated companies throughout the world
www.panmacmillan.com

ISBN 0 330 48815 5

The author gratefully acknowledges the generous support of
the Fondation d'Art de La Napoule: Henry Clews Memorial,
where much of this book was written; and of the University of
the South (Sewanee), whose Tennessee Williams Fellowship
enabled the book's completion.

9 8 7 6 5 4 3 2 1

A CIP catalogue record for this book is available from
the British Library.

Printed and bound in Great Britain by
Mackays of Chatham plc, Chatham, Kent

for Elizabeth

Contents

A Simple Tale

When Maria Poniatowski let herself into Mrs. Ellington's apartment at 7:55 a.m. precisely (she was always five minutes early; she timed her walk that way), on the third Tuesday of August in 1993, and saw, at once, the trail of blood smeared along the wall from the front hall towards the bedroom, she knew that this was the end.

She had come every Tuesday morning—vacations and holidays excepted, and excepting also the still-painful six months in 1991 when Mrs. Ellington had banished her in an inexplicable fit of pique—for forty-six years. She had come, first, to the house on Laurel Heights, and then, when Mrs. Ellington had decamped to the apartment on Manley Avenue in 1977, Maria had come to her there, without missing a beat. And all, thought Maria, with a sudden flush of tears, for the old woman—she was very old now, ninety-two in fact—to be butchered, unsuspecting, in her home. It was too awful. One read about such occurrences in the newspapers (although Maria, not reading English very well, rarely did), or one heard about them on the television. But one did not expect them ever to befall the people that one knew. That's what Maria told herself as she tiptoed along the buff-colored broadloom towards Mrs. Ellington's bedroom.

But in fact she was far more surprised to find Mrs. Ellington snoring softly in her four-poster, propped up by three pillows, her rose satin bed jacket bloodstained but neatly buttoned—far more surprised than she would have been to discover a mangled corpse. Mrs. Ellington's eyes, the milky blue eyes that could no longer see, fluttered open as Maria drew near, and strove, in vain, to focus.

"Is that you? Is that you, Maria?" she asked, her high, brittle voice tinged with panic.

"It's me, Mrs. Ellington," Maria reassured her. "What's been happening here, Mrs. Ellington?"

But Mrs. Ellington, having established the identity of her visitor, slipped swiftly into ill humor. "Dammit," she muttered. "What time is it? That bloody clock. I've overslept. It must be eight. I'll get your coffee, Maria, just hold your horses. For heaven's sake, you might give me a minute . . ." The old woman, her fluffed hair pressed flat at the side of her head, her ravaged hands fumbling with the blankets, hauled herself up and swung her feet to the floor. The bed was high—it was Mrs. Ellington's marriage bed—and Mrs. Ellington was small: her feet dangled a few inches above the carpet, sweeping, like divining rods, in search of her slippers. Maria bent and slid the pink mules one at a time over Mrs. Ellington's scaly insteps.

"I'll get your dressing gown, Mrs. Ellington. No hurry. Take your time."

"Every bloody Tuesday," muttered Mrs. Ellington. "I hope the half-and-half is still good," she said more loudly, "because if it's not, you'll just have to have milk."

"Don't worry, Mrs. Ellington. It's a beautiful day outside."

Mrs. Ellington, stumbling past Maria towards the bathroom, merely grunted.

When they were, at last, in their usual places in the breakfast nook, their usual coffee (Maria's with half-and-half) on the table before them, the sun streaming in so brightly that Mrs. Ellington's blind eyes blinked, Maria raised the subject of the blood on the wall.

At first, Mrs. Ellington did not seem to understand what Maria was talking about. She pursed her lips (over all her own teeth; she was very proud of her teeth) and shook her head. But then she said, "My finger. I cut my finger making dinner. It was the broccoli. I suppose that's it." She held up her left hand to the side of her head, where a sliver of peripheral vision remained to her, and peered at it in grave concentration. "Dammit, I don't know. It's all a blur, Maria. Will you look at it for me?"

Maria took the arthritic digits between her own hands: their forms were gnarled, and the worn skin was shiny, but Mrs. Ellington's hand was soft and faintly tremulous, like a palpitating bird, in Maria's grasp. On Mrs. Ellington's forefinger there was a long, streaked scab. The cut was quite deep: Maria could tell that if she were to give the finger a sharp squeeze, it would start, again, to bleed.

"This is no good, Mrs. Ellington. How can you manage this way? It's so hard. You need help."

"Aren't you my help?"

Maria went, without replying, to fetch disinfectant and a cotton ball. She sighed. She would have to speak to Mrs. Ellington's daughter. But Judith lived in California, and Maria didn't make long-distance calls.

"When is Judith coming?" she asked Mrs. Ellington as she daubed at the finger. "Or Simon? Or Madeleine? Or Kate?"— these were Judith's three children, full-grown themselves, and scattered like chaff across the continent.

"To Toronto?" Mrs. Ellington grimaced, either at the prospect of her descendants gathering or in pain at the stinging of her hand, or both. "Judith said after Labor Day, but I don't know how long after."

"You'll speak to her tonight?" Judith called Mrs. Ellington daily.

"I suppose. If she remembers."

"Of course she remembers." Maria took a deep breath. "Maybe you tell her to call me, ya? I need to talk with her."

"Not about me, you don't," snapped Mrs. Ellington, blinking furiously.

"No, no. Just about things."

Judith was often between them. Maria had known Judith since the latter was fifteen years old. She had witnessed, over the years, many altercations between Mrs. Ellington and her only child, and she had long ago given up trying to take sides.

But when Mrs. Ellington—whose general temper had, in recent years, taken a powerful turn for the worse, as if her good humor had evaporated with her eyesight—had summarily dismissed Maria from her employ with an unprecedented shriek over two years previously, it was Judith who had served as a mediator. She had initially apologized on her mother's behalf, had calmed the old woman sufficiently for Mrs. Ellington to apologize herself, and had facilitated Maria's reentry into the Ellington home. "She can't manage without you, Maria, no matter what she pretends. She's completely lost. I know it's a lot to ask. I know how impossible she is. But if you could find it in your heart—"

And Maria, after six months of empty Tuesdays, almost seventy herself and with no interest in finding a new Tuesday job; after six months in which she had used her newly free time to plant her garden, to paint her kitchen, to repaper her hall, only then to sit and survey her domestic perfection with irritation and ennui, had capitulated. She had had only two households left on her roster, Mrs. Ellington and Jack McDonald and his wife: she'd worked for Jack's parents until they died, and had cleaved, quite naturally, to their son, although she found Elspeth McDonald's smoking displeasing and could not stand their lumbering Labrador, Sport. So that without Mrs. Ellington, Maria had been lonely. She had missed her fractious employer, and the calm rituals of her workday on Manley Avenue: the leisurely coffee, the chattering radio that Mrs. Ellington played constantly, the swift rhythms of vacuuming and dusting, the changing of the sheets. She had missed the particular smells, of Mrs. Ellington's favorite furniture polish, of her bath salts, and the intimate scents of her faintly musty cupboards; and she had missed their shared lunches, after the work was done, the slow, talk-filled afternoon meal of sandwiches (white bread, crusts trimmed, Bick's yum-yum pickles always in a cut glass dish between them at the table) and Fig Newtons and tea. She'd missed the way Mrs. Ellington's voice would rise when she said, "Cup of tea, Maria?" asking politely each time, although Maria had never once in all those years said no; and she missed even the sound of her own voice saying, "Yes please, Mrs. Ellington," and the pleasure of waiting, with her hands in her lap, for that satisfying moment when Mrs. Ellington, so imperious, poured the boiling tea from the flowered pot into her, Maria's, waiting cup.

In short, Mrs. Ellington's apartment was as much a part of Maria's quotidian life as Sunday morning mass, and she returned because her own kitchen bored her, and her house, on Tuesdays, seemed in its shadowy quiet to wish her gone. But then, that August morning, sitting with Mrs. Ellington in the little breakfast nook, with the blood still streaked along the wall in the hallway, Maria felt suddenly that everything was different. All the familiar objects were in their rightful places—the Noah's Ark platter on the wall, the doilies centered neatly beneath the fruit bowl and the tea tray—but Maria was visited again by the choked sensation that she had suffered when she had first opened the apartment door: this was the end.

It had been the same with Bert McDonald, Jack's father, not long after his wife Gail had passed. But Jack had been there; even Elspeth, cigarette in hand, had been there. They had seen for themselves. They had not had to be told. And it wasn't that Mr. McDonald had been so very old; it had been, above all, that he drank. Jack and Elspeth had hustled him into a home with barely any protest on his part, and had visited him there, as Maria had visited him there, every week for four years until he died.

But Mrs. Ellington was not groggy with gin, and she would not, Maria knew, give in without a struggle. She would not be herself, Mrs. Ellington, without the trappings of her life around her. She would say it, and mean it, and it would be true. Besides, part of Maria did not want Mrs. Ellington to give in at all: she was, after all, the last of the first generation, now that the McDonalds (and before them, the Pollocks, and old Mrs. Mallow) were gone. Difficult as she could be, Mrs. Ellington was family.

Not that Maria didn't have family of her own, real family. She'd lost her beloved Lev in '72, but she had her boy Radek, or Rod, as he preferred to be called, and Anita, his wife, and the children, little Paul and Kelly. But they were out in Oakville, and she sometimes didn't see them for months at a time; and they weren't like Mrs. Ellington, they were her descendants, after all. The different parts of Maria's life were like fragments of a broken mirror, and although she could see herself in all of them, she could not make them fit together. How to reconcile that plump and squalling infant of the serious blue gaze, and the fleshy middle-aged Canadian engineer her son had become? The two beings seemed discrete, unconnected one to the other: but Mrs. Ellington, who had seemed old to Maria even then, back in 1947, stout in her sturdy shoes with her grey permanent wave, had merely continued to be old,

9

older but much the same, in one slow consoling sweep of un-
broken time until that August morning.

Maria had been born outside Gulyaypole, in the Ukraine, in a
village where her family had belonged since before records
began. The Soviet Union was young, then, although the village was old; and although restructured as a collective farm, an
administrative alteration of which Maria's parents and uncles
and cousins complained, it was, to all intents and purposes, the
village they had always known. Maria was the eldest of five
children, the third of whom succumbed in infancy to an un-
specified fever (the doctor was a local man, whose training had
taken place *in situ*: even for ailments he recognized, he did
not always have names, and he favored antiquated terms like
"ague" and "malaise" which served at once to professionalize
and to obfuscate his diagnoses), and her cousins numbered, or
so it had felt, in the hundreds. The vast and muddy acreage beyond their village was tilled and tended by relatives of all ages;
for as long as it was possible, the domed brick church—burned,
under Stalin, so that only a monstrous metal cage remained of
its gilded onion—harbored all the villagers together, on Sun-
days and for festivals. The Soviets built a school where formerly none had existed, and Maria and her siblings had, for
several years at least (until the young schoolmaster vanished in
the night and was neither located nor replaced), the benefit of
instruction: they scratched their lessons upon slates in the
sooty fug of the coal-heated classroom, and to the shuffling rub
of their boots they recited verses and sang songs for the glory of
the union.

At home, in their cottage, with its once-white picket fence and once-white shutters—the long-ago vanity of Maria's father, who had purchased the paint on a rare visit to the nearest source, sixteen hard miles distant, and who had never since had sufficient money or leisure to touch up the job—Maria helped her mother as soon as she was able, and once the teacher disappeared, she helped her all day long. The cottage contained three rooms only, in which all seven and then, with the death of her grandmother, six of them huddled, rich in the smells of sweat and coal and cabbage and in the secretive glint of the illicit icon upon one shadowed wall. They walked in socks on the overlapping threadbare rugs, leaving their boots, caked with the viscous orange mud of the region, in the covered porch by the cold spigot. In winter, Maria recalled, the boots would freeze in the night, and present themselves unyielding to her raw and blistered feet. She slept beneath rugs in a straw bed in the central room between her two sisters, head to toe, the three of them warming and crushing one another in the night, which infinite darkness (except, of course, when the moon was on the snow, and a ghostly blue reflection illuminated the room) nursed a multitude of sounds: her father's intermittent belches from next door, behind the curtain; the wheeze of little Dasha's bronchial slumber; the scrambling of the rats that nestled in the foundation; the ticking of the frost on the panes; and, at dawn, the rattle of cousin Pavel's wagon in the rutted dirt road outside. They took meals, too, in the same room, at a slabbed table draped with a yellow oilcloth, and it was, for years, Maria's job to wash the dishes, scoured with a rush whisk at the cold-water tap on the porch. In winter, the rubber hose that fed the tap from the well would freeze, like the boots, and water had to be fetched in the form of snow and melted by the fire.

Maria, many years later, could conjure exactly the stink of the outhouse, and its chinked gloom; she could locate, in her mind's eye, each knot in the wooden door, each filtered sunbeam which caught the dust and illuminated the blue-black wings of the flies that congregated over the shit; just as she could still feel the winter chapping her buttocks as she squatted, straining, over the cesspit; and hear, still, the tinny tinkle as she or her sisters (it was only a woman's right) urinated in the bucket in the corner of the porch on a cold night.

Her sisters' and her brother's faces had grown blurry with the passage of time, but Maria could see precisely, in fragments, the beloved elements of her mother's face: the etched lines across her narrow forehead, beneath the patterned headscarf; the thick black bun at her mother's nape, filigreed with the silver strands that had so impressed her; the rippling creases in her mother's ruddy cheeks when, rarely, she laughed; her mother's almost purple lips, naturally bright as if cherry-stained; and the drooping lobes of her ears, the left longer than the right, from which swung delicate pearl and gold earrings, her dowry and her inheritance. Maria's father had been a slight and wiry man—from him she had inherited her frame—with a broad gap between his front teeth and an anxious expression. He lacked two fingers on his right hand, the fourth and the pinky, lost in an accident with a thresher as a boy. She remembered the nubbed texture of his stumps when she took and held that hand, and the emotion that they had evoked: she had thought him brave, an intrepid survivor, and had long and proudly believed his injuries to be war wounds.

She remembered, too, the vastness of the sky, the afternoons when, at the edge of the village, she would look out and up at a landscape shaded between black and white: the grey white of the expanse of cloud, pregnant with snow, the white white of the drifts, the black trunks of trees and shrubs and the dark runnels of loam among the glistening fields. Into this wide, flat plain, a horse-drawn sleigh might slide, jangling; or a black dog, bandy-legged, goitered, might saunter along the black and white road. In Maria's memories of childhood, the vision was very often invernal, although she had lived as many summers in her parents' house as she had winters.

She could not revisit the time in between the rumor of war and its arrival. War had been visited upon them first as famine, a war merely to survive the bitter winter months. Crops had failed: the barns that should have been heaped with grain were home only to gaunt rats and the wind whispering amid the chaff along the floor. Then there were no rats, even. The few cows, as the winter proceeded, shrank to bone, and the horses too, until they were all eaten and their bones boiled. The kolkhoz which had been a village was a community linked, then, above all in suffering: everybody came to look related, whether they were or not, conjoined in the hollowing of their eyes and the press of their bones against their skin. They ate grass soup. With slingshots, Maria and her siblings tried to kill the rare crows that speckled the white drifted landscape, and only once succeeded. They ate even the cats. Then there was nothing left at all: the war came in person, and was almost a relief.

Maria was nearly fifteen when the Germans arrived in Gulyaypole. Spring was on its way, and the ground sinking from snow into rivers of orange mud. The soldiers with their fishbone gutturals had had mud upon their boots, mud thick as a cast upon their uniforms up to their knees. They had not been brutal—there were enough, in the region, who could trace German ancestry, fair Ukrainian peasants named Otto and Fritz—but they had not bent, either. In her last days in her parents' house, Maria shared the main room with her mother and father, while two German soldiers slept in their bed. Maria recalled one of them, hardly her senior, as handsome, with silvery blond hair, sallow skin and voluptuous, protuberant lips like a Pole.

She could not have said whether she had cried upon quitting her family; it had not seemed, as they boarded the trucks, like the end. And in fact perhaps she had mused, in her adolescent heart, upon the prospect of romance with the sallow blond, of a prosperous and early marriage; even in the hard time, she had been, she was the first to admit it, a frivolous girl, conscious of her dark good looks, the rose of her cheeks (albeit from hunger and cold rather than health) and the twinkle of gold at her ears. She had known the timbre of her laugh to be pretty, even if the Germans could not understand her speech. Let it be said that the soldiers were civil; they presented departure as a choice, an invitation, although everyone tacitly knew that it was not. They left all the old people (Maria's mother, not yet then thirty-five, was too antique for their notice) to wave mournfully in the mud, kerchiefs clutched at the chin, caps off, the children frolicking around as if at a festival, Maria's brother and youngest sister among them. But Dasha and Maria, at thirteen and almost fifteen, had boarded the trucks as if it were a choice, as did all their friends, and several of their cousins, with only the clothes on their backs, and when Maria remembered that morning it was not people, nor the village, that returned: it was the smell of diesel, strong as ten tractors, and the splintering needles of the early spring sleet, and overhead, and infinite, the billowing sky, not white, not blue, but a shroud of terrible grey.

Not long in the first camp, Maria had there been separated from her sister, from her cousins, and from all but one friend. It was only then that she had felt this truly to be departure, and by then it was too late to cry. She was grateful, at least, for Olga, her companion, a gay, solid girl of seventeen, whose braids were as blond as Maria's were black, who was favored by the Germans therefore, and who swore, by the blood of her pricked finger (she was unafraid, at least then, was Olga) that she would not suffer their pair to be parted. And then, with Olga, by train this time, Maria was shunted north and west, closer to Germany.

They were crammed into boxcars that stank of shit, and although there was space enough to sit, knees cramped to the chin, there was no room to lie down. There were water stops, though, and there was bread, thrown through the cracked door in the stations along the way, bread that tasted delicious for being bread at all.

Let it be clear: they were not prisoners. So they were told, although they did not have a choice. They were laborers. Had there been a limit to their servitude, they might have been termed indentured servants. They were not well treated; the inefficient and the sickly among them were beaten, or left for dead, or sent elsewhere for efficient extermination. But they were not Jews, nor were they political insurgents, nor Gypsies nor homosexuals. They were peasants, labeled with the word "OST" stitched in blue to their breasts, signifying their provenance, hoarded in barracks with others like themselves, strong-backed and sturdy-limbed, culled from villages and farms across the conquered territories, not quite starved, and yoked, like oxen, for the glory of the Reich.

From the camp where they were housed, they were loaded onto trucks in the mornings before dawn and taken out to work the fields, to hoe and to weed, eventually to sow, endless hours of backbreaking toil that blistered their palms and coated their skin in runnels of sweat. They had only half an hour at noon to rest in the pounding sun, and only bread and water to assuage the gnaw of their innards. Their evening meal was a gristle-laced broth and a cup of chicory swill, so that weekly their clothes, tattering anyway, hung more loosely around them.

Olga and Maria were vain, and hopeful in spite of everything, and they contrived to manufacture blusher of red clay dug surreptitiously from the banks of the stream, to beg the stubs of matchsticks with which to darken their eyes. They were as scrupulous in their cleanliness as the conditions allowed, and once a week they would don their washed clothes in the morning, still damp, to dry on their backs while they worked.

They had no news of their village, nor of their siblings nor cousins nor friends, and so were able to imagine that time, in

Gulyaypole, had stood still, and to bicker over which of them would ensnare the coveted local champion upon their return, and to debate the merits of building new houses for their families or inheriting the old. (How could they have known, then, that all the boys and young men who had shared their trucks, their champion among them, had been sewn, straightaway, into the striped uniforms of convicts, and sent to die blasting tunnels in the north, near Poland?) Olga and Maria shared a tittering *faiblesse* for the camp's lame dentist, a chiseled and dashing graduate from Belgrade whose gimp had spared him the fate of their own menfolk, but whose talents with pliers had ensured, for the time being at least, his life. As was the fashion, then, among the camp's girls, Maria removed the precious gold earrings from her lobes and paid this gentleman to cap her incisors with silver: it was thought to enhance her already pretty smile (and even so many years later, as she looked in the mirror, Maria derived pleasure from the glimmer of her grin, and this although the fashion, local to begin with, had long waned; and her Canadian dentist, aghast, had for years begged to remove them). Olga, too, would have done the same; but she felt that with her coloring only gold would serve, and found that in the dentist's eyes her trinkets were insufficient payment.

As for the endless hours in the mucky fields, barked at and prodded with sticks, as for the lice, as for the protruding xylophones that were their ribs, Maria, so long afterwards, could barely recall them. Olga and she had marched, and then trudged, and then gasped through those days (weeks, months) with their eyes (their charcoaled eyes) so firmly on the mirage of release, on the hallucinated oasis of Gulyaypole, that Maria had excised, from her life's recording, all but the most abbreviated and clouded impressions of their first labor camp. The clay, the kohl, the dentist: these things, along with the firm fair hand of Olga, and the bristling tickle of her blond braid against Maria's cheek, were all that really remained, like the scattering of items on the memory-game tray at a children's birthday party.

Olga would have remembered more, perhaps; but where was Olga? She might still have been living, in 1993, somewhere—anywhere: in Australia, or in America, or in Toronto itself; or even in Gulyaypole. It was possible, although not, Maria knew, with their beloved champion, the rumor of whose early death had reached her, along with those of so many others, at some indistinguishable moment in the war. Maria did not aspire to a reunion with Olga: their looks were gone, even if her own silver teeth remained, and they would not, were they to retrieve one another, recapture the brutal willed optimism that had sustained them there: if anything, they would weep, and Maria had, between Mrs. Ellington, the McDonalds, her house and her family, no time for fruitless tears over what was lost. Olga was like a beautiful poppy in the muck of a waste ground, and even if she passed Olga every day on Bloor Street or in the crowd at Honest Ed's discount store, Maria didn't want to know it.

After the camp, delightfully rustic in comparison to what followed (there were at least birds, and the sound of water), Maria had been separated from her stalwart companion (in spite of the blood promise: what was a pinpricked thumb next to the threat of extermination?) and taken to Essen, the heart of the enemy. There, alongside countless rows of other girls, from all over, a veritable Tower of Babel, reduced to the Esperanto of signs and grimaces, beneath signs that read (had Maria been able to read) "Slawen Sind Sklawen," Slavs are Slaves, Maria was set to work for Krupps, the master munitions maker, deviser of Fat Gustav, the massive gun that had, not so long before, laid waste to Sevastopol. Her body hunched and frozen, her hands repeated, in unending concatenation, the same three gestures (push, turn, pull) for twelve hours of each day. Where was the choice for them now?

The barracks, wound around with the shimmer, then the rust, of barbed wire, in some satanic parody of festive decoration, lay forty minutes' walk from the factory, along the cobbled streets of Essen. Maria could still hear the clatter of wooden clogs along the pavement in the misty dawn, endless crocodiles of women shivering and ragged; and could still smell the wet, lice-filled blanket she wrapped over herself against the cold. A Krupps blanket, marked by three interlocking wheels, it was also her bedcovering at night, always damp, ever filthier, its smell rank and full. The barracks were darker, narrower, stinking of the few overflowing toilets and infested with vermin.

Then, in the spring of '43, the bombings came, a thunder that erupted and never again stopped. Thereafter, the sky, when glimpsed, was small and menacing, carrying too often upon its chill breezes the whir of enemy—of Allied—bombers. There was no Olga, there was no longer any Gulyaypole. For Maria, there, in the tunneled existence, the mechanical push merely to survive, a drone among faceless drones, the past and the future fell away. In their stead, she experienced fear; and as the war bore on, and the bombings—spectacular, shattering, apocalyptic bombings—intensified, it came to seem that these eruptions were not merely the source of her fear, but her fear itself. She did not think in terms of liberation, or in terms of enemies and allies; and she did not think, any longer, in terms of her girlish beauty and the prospect of love. Insofar as was possible, she did not think, and in this she was aided by the reverberating factory machines by day and the reverberating bombs by night. There were no underground bunkers for the laborers, deemed replaceable in the event of a hit—they had only trenches, slits they dug for themselves in the mud—and their munitions factory was of course a target: Maria breathed in fear of death.

Barracks upon barracks were flattened: women and girls she had come to know by sight, and some she knew better than that, vanished from one day to the next, swallowed by the night's newly born, voracious rubble. Inevitably came the night when her own building burst, a splintered crater all that remained in the smoke-filled dawn; and the women, her group, were consigned instead to a cellar, without light or water, or even beds, so that they slept huddled in their blankets on the icy ground.

When the young woman beside her on the assembly line, in a few broken words and the language of gestures, proposed flight, Maria did not hesitate. The woman was Romanian, from the countryside, and built as though she ought to have been zaftig; but the years of privation had rendered her big-boned and gaunt. Her wrists and ankles bulged like vast bolts. Her face was still round as a plate, her skin without pores, and her eyes were very pale, the color of clear water. Her dark hair, which ought, too, to have been her glory, was hacked above her ears as if in mourning; and she never smiled. Her name was Dardia.

They fled at night, the two of them. In the middle of a raid, in a blackout, it was not so difficult after all (did they not, officially at least, have a choice?): the guards squirreled below-ground, and beyond the factory walls, in the ravaged streets of the city (it was late in the war, by now), there was no one—the citizens, too, were *sub terra*, or else cowering in corners behind veils of black felt, praying that the explosions would not find them.

Maria and Dardia scurried aboveground when the droning began, slipped out of the cellar as the other women hunkered down in the invisible blackness, and crouched together in the rain of bombs, in the occasional light of fiery explosion, watching the billowing world around them reconfigure, grow strange, disappear and reemerge in the murky cacophony. Nothing would ever compare to that terror: Maria never spoke of it, but thought of it, to herself, as the endless suspended moment that she lived *in death*. These were the only words she could conceive to contain that night, that chasm of fear and the liberation, with it, of being beyond. Having squatted among the bombs, holding Dardia's clammy hand in her own, their sweat running together in the cold night, she could never have gone back. Only forward. And as if there were a God, the nearest explosion had blown a gaping rent in the electrified fence—its electricity dead at last—and the two girls had stepped forward, as if called, and climbed through the swirling, choking smoke into the street outside.

The town, in the fugged blackness, did not look familiar, although they had trudged its thoroughfares, factory-bound, for so long. Maria and Dardia could not tell in which direction they walked, and perhaps they walked in circles, because it seemed they wandered for hours without ever nearing the open ground that would signal the end of Essen. When first light poked greyly through the mist, they found themselves surrounded on both sides by Essen's dead, by the cemeteries on Segerothstrasse, and when they caught the first tickings and slammings of Germans emerging from their shelters, the girls darted among the broken tombstones and flattened themselves in the long grasses of the town's untended Jewish graves. Without even their blankets, stuck numb to the ground, they lay till nightfall, till the Allied buzz echoed once again from the horizon; and while they hid, famished, thirsty, they listened like hounds to the human movement—the clank and clatter, the rolling of occasional trucks along the Strasse—to try to gauge which route led out of their hell, and away. In the newly bomb-bloomed night, they stopped by the banks of the canal to drink, cupping their stiff hands and slurping greedily, indifferent in their thirst to what poisons the rubbish-filled water might carry; then headed north without knowing it, until they broke, in the darkness, the town's limits.

For three nights, the two girls pressed northwards, to the Rhine and beyond. They turned away from roads or scuttled across them doubled over, and hid by day in barns or woods, foraging in pig slop or gnawing at roots and fungi among the trees. It was a dreamscape: it was springtime, and a frost fell, still, near dawn, upon the air. But, as in dreams, water presented itself when they most required it, at a well or from a brook, and some form of sustenance loomed miraculous just when it seemed they could push no further (they had been trained, after all, for a long time to require little); and as in dreams, they started at dogs' barks, at engines or, once, at approaching footsteps, and yet managed somehow to render themselves invisible, camouflaged by scrawniness and by their supreme quiet. The two girls could not speak, or hardly, and so did not, picking their way, night and day, in this silence that rendered their journey all the more surreal.

Maria did not choose to remember that time, although her mind had so clearly recorded it, because, until the farmer, the journey was an icy cascade of fear. Her body remembered it best, and reminded her, still, sometimes, in spring, near dawn, when the window was open to the cold dew, and she juddered awake in her Markham Street bed, clutching at the blanket and for her husband (he, too, now long gone), her heart like a knocked pipe, seemingly audible throughout the house, and calmed only as she fixed, object by soothing object, on the contents of her room.

When the farmer found them, on the third day or the fourth, that too had felt like a dream. At first, in truth, like a nightmare. They had, both of them, been soundly and exhaustedly asleep in a ditch, beneath his hedgerow: at sunrise, when they had stopped their walk, they had seen no house upon the horizon, and so had thought themselves safe. It was but a few short hours later that his German shepherd, all ears, snout and fangs, in great excitement pawed them awake into the horror of discovery they had, from the first, imagined. Dardia opened her mouth to scream, but no sound emerged (it was as if they had dwelt too long in silence), and Maria raised her hands above her shoulders in a gesture of surrender. The farmer appeared first as a raucous shout that calmed the dog, and then in silhouette, a huge black blot bearing a staff before the sun. He barked at them in German, the very sounds of which had gutted the air. But when they stood, in their tattered overalls, their hair matted with leaves and sticks, their grimed hands aloft, they could see that he was in fact small and old, and a peasant like themselves.

Eventually it emerged, through force of largely extra-linguistic effort, where they originally hailed from; and indeed, it was revealed that he, a veteran of the Kaiser's army in his youth, had been stationed in Slovenia and had suffered there the grand passion of his life. For this, he took pity on them. He recognized them for what they were, Balkan milkmaids, as he called them, and assured that they were neither Gypsy nor Jew, he and his tiny, barrel-bellied wife agreed to hide them in return for much-needed assistance on the farm. Earlier in the war, they had had workers from the East, two girls with the same "OST" labels on their breasts; but the Reich had reclaimed them, for the factories, for Krupps. Their sons were gone to war, one dead, one on the Russian front and the third unheard from for months; and their daughter had, several years before, married a Bavarian billeted briefly nearby and decamped, when his platoon had left, to the unseen home of her in-laws.

Maria and Dardia were both farm girls by birth, and could hoe and milk and harvest and spin and sew. Clad in clothes left behind by the married daughter, shod still in their clumsy regulation clogs, they found a measure of peace on their German farm, above which the bombers flew only irregularly and high, as muted as gnats. As the weather grew warmer they could roll up their sleeves and sing while they worked, taking turns, one eerie, mournful keening after another, that reminded them, perhaps too much, of home. Rooted in the present, the farmer's wife taught them the German words they needed, for butter and beer and bread, for calf and pig. She had them sleep in her sons' room, a gabled nest under the eaves which smelled always of verbena soap, with the boys' photographs proud upon the wall; and she kept a sprig of green, or a blooming flower always in a vase before the image of her dead eldest. When word came that the third boy, too, was gone, she put out vases for all three: two in memoriam and one, apparently, as a preventative measure.

With the advantage of milk and eggs, and the blessing of a soft, clean bed, the girls also began to bloom again. The gloss returned to their hair and the smile to Dardia's stony face. They were able to forget, for a time, about the war, which was, if they had known it, coming to its close; and in their dovetailed farm-house rhythms, Maria and Dardia behaved, and seemed, to the pleasure of their hosts, like sisters. The farm, as Maria could still see it, a low, neat cottage with red geraniums outside the windows, had a particular light around it, the misted glow of early morning or late afternoon, and she pictured the farmer and his wife in her apron at the door, waving, waving, with true tears upon their withered cheeks.

Because when the foreigners in their unfamiliar uniforms, with their unfamiliar linguistic cacophonies, came rolling through the fallen Reich, Maria and the now reluctant Dardia were prodded, gathered, and set on the move once more. It was, then, a kind of an end; but not the end at all. The beginning of something else. Yet another encampment: and what, finally, was the difference (aside from better and more abundant food, and relative cleanliness, and medical care) between one camp and another? This was the liberators' camp, so-called, and Maria and her ilk were now termed "Displaced Persons"; but it was a camp nonetheless, with bunks and a rodent-filled mess and a wire fence all the same; and they had no more the right to leave this one than they had any of the others.

Once there, and catalogued, Maria and Dardia, till then so much like sisters, had barely spoken, and ultimately had parted without farewells. This was not so strange: they had shared a journey, and a sojourn; they had been *in death* together; but this new life's fragment they would not share. Dardia, like the farm, the factory, Olga, the camp and Gulyaypole, became part of Maria's past, figments, stored, quietly, away. With Dardia went the few German words Maria had learned (she would not acknowledge them, so many years later, at the German butcher's in Toronto's West End, when she heard the stout owner calling his son for more cheese, more cream, from the storeroom); there began another way of speaking.

And finally there, in the Displaced Persons camp, Maria, an old maid of twenty who thought her looks spoiled (except, of course, for the silver glimmer of her incisors), had her love story. At long last. Dreamed, discarded, forgotten, it came to her on the sly, slowly at first, shy, and then in full torrent. That's what the Displaced Persons camp would mean to her, in the ribbon of years: simply, love.

Lev was five years older than Maria. Fair, sallow, with pro-truberant lips, he was her Pole. He was tall, too, and angular, with large, spatulate hands and veined limbs: when she saw his legs bare, she could trace upon them, beneath the blond down, the circuitry and byways of his most insignificant bloodlines, raised blue and mauve filaments like industrial wiring. He was so skinny as to be hollow, but that hollow, in their embraces, proved her nest: his arms would fold around her and Maria would imagine herself tented, wholly cocooned in the warm salt smell of him, a smell of sweat that was uniquely his, sharper and cleaner, she felt, for his blondness. They spoke Russian at first, a broken, schooled language for both of them, the language of Stalin, and then taught one another the endearments of their native tongues; but they were learning English, too, and in time they spoke of everything but love in this new speech, in part be-cause it had no past for them and hence carried no pain, and in part because they decided, together, to choose Canada.

Again, choice was but a semblance: they could have opted to return whence, long before, they had come, but to return to-gether to Poland or the Ukraine, to lives as wrecked and for-lorn as the skeleton dome of the church in Gulyaypole, did not seem, in the Soviet light, possible. Once they were married— by a British military minister, whose Anglican profession bore little connection to the Catholicism of Lev's youth, nor to Maria's clandestine Orthodoxy—they wanted only to press forward; all the more so after the nine months that brought Radek, pale, solemn and screaming, to them; and to press for-ward meant to push out of Europe, away from the shrouded skies and the past.

This seemed, to the British and Canadian camp administrators, like a decision of perfect logic. Those who had ventured from the new world back to the rubble of the old, to offer succor and assistance, were full of the promises of their origins: well-fed, buffed, eyes alight, these men and occasional women extolled North America's virtues, the plenty, the illumination, the cleanliness of it.

"You can have a whole house," said one, a mere boy, with his eyes damp at the memory of his parental hearth. "Made of brick or of wood, as you choose. With central heating and running water, with two or three floors, and a garden for flowers. And you can find jobs, no problem: North America's full of jobs. It's the land of opportunity. The land of the future."

They listened, Lev and Maria, and they discussed the matter in their quarters (a double cot, curtained only by hanging laundry from neighboring double cots, in an enforced intimacy which, at night, in its ripe airlessness and breathy sounds, recalled to Maria her own childhood home), while Radek suckled peaceably at Maria's breast, swaddled in an army issue blanket of rough grey wool. And they came, in their mottled new language cobbled of all their languages (except German; they never used German words), to the conclusion that it was best to take the leap.

If Maria had not met Lev, had not given birth to Radek; if indeed, she had rediscovered Olga and her blond braids, then she might have made her way home to Gulyaypole: but none of her fellows in the camp brought any word of sisters or cousins or friends, and it seemed that Gulyaypole had perhaps been obliterated, had simply ceased to exist. Like Lot's wife, Maria was at moments tempted to turn back, to look for her past; but she knew the price, with a husband and a son to care for, to be too high. In the event, she paid a public scribe to write a letter to her parents (if her parents were indeed still alive) knowing that they, too, would pay, if they received it, to have it deciphered for them; and she set the envelope in the hands of a Canadian soldier with as little confidence as if she were setting a bottle to bob upon the open sea. All that she said in this letter, in the formal constructions of the pedant who penned it, a diction not at all her own, was that she was well, and in Germany, with a Polish spouse and a baby, and that she was headed to America (Canada, the United States—what difference did these names make to her then? And what difference could they make to her parents?). She would write again, she informed them, from there, where she would have a house and a garden, perhaps a cow and a horse, or a goat, of her own.

Lev, who spoke little of his past but whose war, she surmised from his silence and from the sorrow in the angles of his hollow bones, had been far worse than her own, had nobody to whom to signal his departure. He had known his parents to be dead for some years, and had seen his only brother slaughtered before his eyes: he did not explain where, or when, or how, but Maria pictured a ditch, and snow, and into her nightmare image sauntered the black goitered dog of her memories of Gulyaypole. Nothing more was said on the subject.

Finally, eventually, they crossed by sea, clutching their new papers (which they could not read, as they were in English) and enduring the disconsolate squalls of their son who, too small still to walk, failed also, as expression would have it, to find his sea legs. He vomited bile and shrieked at the ocean, sick above deck as below. Each morning they asked how much longer to Halifax, and each morning it seemed that the sailors, chipper and jaunty in anticipation of home, offered the empty promise of "Not long now."

From Halifax, once they arrived, the Poniatowskis were escorted, in the company of their fellow DPs (once in Canada, they were referred to by initials only, as DPs), across the continent westwards, by train, as far as Ontario. Lev and Maria had understood, more or less, before embarking, that their relocation entailed a temporary commitment to the Canadian nation—"A real short time," the camp administrator in Germany had assured them, "kind of earning your crossing, you know?"—but they were still taken aback by their arrival, after dark, by bus, at a manned gate, official entrance to a cluster of low-slung, primitive buildings scattered among the pines, that recognizably formed a camp: a loggers' camp. By now, one way or another, Maria knew what a camp looked like.

Their first night at Tagomack, in the wooded backlands of northern Ontario just east of Sudbury, settled into an institutional flatlet that was, in fact, half of a tarpaper cabin, with a kitchenette, a sitting room piled with old magazines they could not read, and a small bedroom at the back, with a window into complete blackness—that first night, Maria wept.

"It's all a lie!" she sobbed in Ukrainian, as Lev looked on with a stricken expression, Radek blinking soberly in the crook of his arm. "We'll be trapped in the camps forever! And they told us the war was over—a lie!"

But by day, the prospect was less intolerable: their cabin had hot and cold running water, the shower rooms were properly heated, and the breakfast provided from vast steaming trays in the mess hall was more copious than any meal Maria had seen since early childhood, and then only at festivals: there were pork sausages and rashers of bacon, eggs and toast, both white bread and brown, and grilled tomatoes, tinned mushrooms, baked beans (Maria, later to become an aficionado, had never yet, at that juncture, confronted baked beans) and pancakes, and, for these latter, a plethora of condiments, margarine and strawberry jam, lemon, white sugar, and a thick, treacly syrup.

Besides, in the morning, that first September morning of 1946, there was the piercing early-autumn sunlight sifting through the pines, and the clean odor of the needles as they were trampled underfoot, and the soft damp mulch scent of the forest; and there were maples, in amongst the monstrous evergreens, turning, golden, vermilion, ochre in a riotous celebration of the Poniatowskis' arrival. Little Radek, seduced by the colors, reached his grasping paw towards the heavens, to try to contain the light. And again: the bedroom window which, the night before, had seemed through its flimsy blind to give onto the void, opened, in fact, upon a quiet grove of birches, familiar to Maria from her childhood, with their lean, blanched, peeling trunks and shimmering leaves; and through them stole the gleam of blue water: a hidden lake which, upon closer inspection, would prove profound and crystalline, its ancient lichened rockbed three men deep, appearing close enough to touch.

This camp, the last camp (now, surely, this was the end?) would be their home for nine months. Radek would learn to walk there, and to speak, at least to babble, his first sounds already strangely tongued and gummed, Canadian to his mother's ears. Maria was not unhappy in Tagomack, although sometimes she was bored: Lev, along with the other DP men, an odd assortment of ages and nationalities and physiques, was out of her way from dawn until dusk, and returned before supper, taciturn and weary, his government-issue flannel shirt sawdusted and stiff across the shoulders, his pale hair flattened by the regulation logger's cap, and his spatulate hands raw and callused.

Maria's duties, along with the other women, were in the kitchen and the laundry, peeling buckets of potatoes for the men's evening stews, and stirring pots of boiling linens that they hung, on taut wires, between the trees to dry. During the late afternoons, when the women's work was done, the camp administrators' wives provided domestic education, occasional colloquies on how to shop in a supermarket (for which a special excursion to Sudbury was organized) or on how to calculate weight in pounds and ounces; or, more systematically, the wives provided English classes in speaking, reading and writing, which Maria attended when she was able; but she was slow to befriend other DP women (this was a camp largely of men; there were not many wives, hardly any of Maria's own age, and fewer still with children), so had almost exclusive responsibility for her rambunctious son, and could steal the time only intermittently. She had the alphabet, within nine months, and could write her own, her husband's and her son's names, in a whimsical medley of lowercase and capital letters; but in truth she found it hard to listen to the crisp, haughty inflections of Edith Whitby, the camp administrator's wife, a matron of fifty with rigorous corsetry and uplift whose very bosom seemed to point accusingly at Maria and denounce her insufficient progress; and Maria found that as her speech, already well under way, with Lev, under the tutelage of the military back in Germany, seemed so easily and almost magically to convey her meaning, she had little inclination for written scholarship. After the Tagomack months, she would not study English, not formally—she would not study, indeed, again, but would float, like an unsaved soul, between various analphabetisms, getting by, pretty well, on the spoken and approximated word.

In May, at the end of their tenure—after the long, northern winter of packed snow and blanketing, during which, for the bitter enclosed weeks from December until March, there had been no work for the DPs to do, and after the longer spring of thawing and black flies, when the early forest flowers had bloomed and been plucked by Maria for bedside posies—the Poniatowskis were esteemed ready to be Canadians. The trio of them, clad and shod by the government, had paid their way into society by the sweat of Lev's sallow brow, and more: the savings left over from Lev's labors, and from the neat sewing work that Maria had taken in, for the seemingly interminable winter evenings, had been stored in a Royal Bank of Canada account on their behalf, so that with the official documents, and with their freedom ("so perhaps it isn't a lie?" Maria suggested to her husband, this time with a sly silver-toothed smile), the Poniatowskis were also entrusted with a navy vinyl bankbook in a clear plastic case, showing seven hundred and forty-three dollars and change, recorded, typewritten, in both of their names.

With Radek on his father's lap, the three took the bus—the Greyhound bus, this time, their tickets paid for by themselves, and their traveling companions, as Maria noted with a nudge of Lev's elbow, true Canadians—from the stop outside Rube's coffee shop in downtown Sudbury, to Toronto, the destination upon which they had settled some time before.

Mr. and Mrs. Whitby, the firm hands of Tagomack, were, for all Maria had flinched at Edith's manner, eternally to be thanked for their assistance to the Poniatowskis. The Whitbys did not see fit to help every DP they oversaw so liberally, and so perhaps it was the plump cheeks of little Radek, who might become, yet, a true Canadian; or perhaps it was Maria and Lev's comparative youth, the idea that they might "make a go of it"; or perhaps it was the exceptional quality of Maria's darning (she must have repaired twenty pairs of Whitby socks, not to mention her clever, nearly invisible mending of the moth holes in Edith Whitby's crimson cashmere twinset, from Timothy Eaton's store, if you please). Whatever the reason, the Whitbys furnished both Lev and Maria with fruitful letters of introduction, Lev for construction work at Davidson's in the East End, and Maria for domestic service (and yet, it was again pretended that she had a choice) to a Mrs. Inessa Makerevich in tony Forest Hill.

Mrs. Makerevich, herself a Russian Jew whose parents had had the nous to emigrate when she was just a little girl, before even the great Revolution, took a particular interest in DPs from Eastern Europe. "Poor darlings," she was known, quite erroneously, to exclaim, "I know exactly what it's like!" And more accurately: "Given that I'm all set up now, lending a hand is the least I can do." As small in stature as Maria, she was a buxom bottle blonde who favored tight tweed suits, mink stoles and lipstick, who wore gloves at the wheel of her chocolate-colored Jaguar and who loved to entertain. She already had a DP ("Albanian, or Romanian or something") cooking in her kitchen, and another two to share the housework, but, as she said to Maria, "I like the look of you. A serious girl"—she said it "gel," in Anglophile affectation—"and I'm sure I'll find you something. Rig a jig jig. You can help me out for parties, in the meantime; but I'll get my Leah to spread the word at school, and we'll have you placed in no time. Before, as we say here in Canada, you can say Jack Robinson."

When Maria, uneasy in her one fine blouse and only skirt, secondhand and just a wee bit shiny (from Edith Whitby's closet and nipped a good four inches at the waist by Maria's own expert needle), failed to smile at this, Inessa Makerevich slapped her lightly, confidentially, upon the wrist, and said, with a giggle, "It's an expression, my dear girl. It just means 'fast.' Before you can say Jack Robinson! Rig a jig jig! Presto—voilà!" And to Maria's wary curl of the lip in what might have been a smile and might have been a snarl, she shook her head in mock sorrow: "It's so hard—don't I know it. An immigrant myself. But you'll get the hang of it, poor darling, don't worry."

For two months, while Lev took up hard-hat labor on a site near the harbor, Maria made do with occasional receptions chez Makerevich, frocked and capped in rented black and white ("I'd buy it for you, dear," said Mrs. Inessa, "but it just isn't worth it when you're bound to leave me"). She stood in the Makerevich drawing room, doily-covered tray in hand, passing out tiny lace napkins with which the guests might dab their chins and inhaling their expensive perfumes, and she marveled.

She could not properly tell Lev about what she saw on these evenings, because he had never, in all of his life, witnessed such things, and so could not have imagined them, all gilt and frippery and excess. She marveled, too, that no visible mark of her own life was apparent upon her (excepting, perhaps, her silver incisors; but she did not, at such events, have any call to reveal them), that these men and women could not smell, from her olive skin, the stink of the camps (of camp upon camp) nor detect the ache of nights spent in German ditches, or even the more recent outlines of Tagomack's brutal winter in her bones. But she was, and remained, to the Makerevich entourage, a cipher bearing canapés, a bobbing, black-haired servant whose invisibility was the mark of her professional success, and whose tacit contract with her mistress was to reveal neither past nor present. Even with her fellow maids, Maria discovered, there was no inclination (and not surprisingly: she herself felt none) to discuss what might have come before, but only an urgent need to share the gossip of a newcomer's Toronto: where chicken necks might be had for pennies, out at Royce Dupont; where apartments could be rented, cash on the barrelhead, at a discount; and where, of a free evening (Maria had none), a single girl (which she was not, and hence her lack of freedom) might make connections, seek amusement and conceivably a solid Canadian spouse.

For over two months, during which the Poniatowskis inhabited a singled rented room, with facilities and kitchen on the landing, in a boardinghouse down by the West End tram terminus, these irregular entertainments provided Maria's small portion of income. It was young Leah Makerevich who found her work, in time. Leah, dispatched to a private girls' school every morning through the end of June, in her sailor's middy and pleated skirt; and thereafter, in July, for six weeks, to a summer camp in Muskoka not so far from, nor so very unlike, the Whitbys' Tagomack—except that instead of logging and laundry the girls were inducted into sailing and macramé, with hearty singsongs nightly round a campfire; and the cabins which had seemed to Maria and Lev so luxurious were, to Leah and her ilk, a charming experiment in rustic discomfort—young Leah Makerevich was as dogged as her mother, and when she returned home, mid-August, with a roster of new friends (she, like Maria's long-lost Olga, had been engaged in blood-sisterhood, pricking her pristine thumb), Judith Ellington was among them.

Judith's father, an entrepreneur of theretofore only modest success, had recently and at last succeeded in securing his finances, to the relief of his aspirant and socially frustrated wife. She—none other than Mrs. Brice Ellington—made swift adjustment to the change in their circumstances, enrolling her only child for September in the same private school as Leah (this imminent proximity had, in part, prompted the girls' summer camp bond) and announcing that, for the first time, a cleaning lady was essential to the upkeep of the Ellington home on Laurel Heights.

By strange luck, Mrs. Makerevich herself encountered Gail McDonald at a bridge party at around the same time, and so it was that Maria Poniatowski made these two most lasting connections simultaneously. Others were to follow: Mrs. Mallow lived further down Laurel Avenue, next to the large, gated house that sat mostly empty and was owned, said Mrs. Ellington, by an Arab

CLAIRE MESSUD

(she said it "Ay-rab," and thereby infused that single word with her lingering mistrust of an entire race and a millennium of culture), and learned of Maria's superlative talents at the IGA supermarket on Bloor Street, shaking canteloupes side by side with Mrs. Ellington. Mrs. Mallow was already a widow then, in 1947, and if Mrs. Ellington seemed old to Maria, her neighbor appeared positively antique, with powdery jowls and a slight stoop, and a spreading mole on her left cheek, like a rot, from which several coarse hairs sprouted. The Pollocks Maria met through Mrs. McDonald, as justice dictated, and with this lineup of households she found her weeks more than full.

She went to the McDonalds on Mondays and Wednesdays all day (they had three children—Jack among them, then a boy of nine—who made quite a mess), and to the Ellingtons on Tuesdays until just after lunch. The Pollocks were on Thursdays, once again through till six o'clock (instead of children, Mrs. Pollock kept a pair of small, long-haired white dogs, with smashed noses and Oriental eyes, who shed indiscriminately and whose chronic, vindictive ill temper created a great need for cleaning: when crossed, they vomited and peed and pooped in tantrum (and occasionally in tandem), and when left alone scratched irritably at door frames, piano legs and upholstery, almost as if they were cats). Fridays, Maria saved for Mrs. Mallow, a genuine half-day—home by 2 p.m.—spent largely, it seemed, in keeping the old woman company, as she kept her house pristine of her own accord.

Nobody, now that it was past, wanted to talk about the war. Only Mrs. Mallow mentioned it, in connection with the photo-

38

graph, on her mantel, of her nephew Merlin, an air force pilot shot down over Germany. Maria, upon learning of this loss (Mrs. Mallow's powdered face was streaked by a lone, gentle tear in the telling), heard again the whining bombers, the menacing approach of their engines; but did not feel it appropriate to mention that she had been below, and had hoped, at the time, that men such as Merlin might be plucked, like pheasant, from the skies. In general, she knew that her employers felt an unspoken pity for her unspoken suffering; that they considered, at least initially, their employment of a Displaced Person to be a moral act; and yet, that, unable to imagine her provenance and unwilling to consider it anything other than benighted, they required her silence about her previous life as much as, if not more so than, they required her promptness and efficiency in the acquittal of their household chores.

By force of this silence—it was not, after all, a past that she shared with Lev, either, and their mutual past in the camps did not seem worth saving, when they had a future to build together in Canada—Maria's early fragments drifted from sight, covered over by the daily business of living, an ever more substantial accretion which made, over time, its own past, a Canadian one, in English. Maria was good at her job, conscientious and hardworking, and Lev was industrious also. They had Radek to flutter over, to delight in, as his chubby limbs lengthened and refined themselves into the ebullient form of a boy, a Canadian boy just as the Whitbys would have wished, with a little bully's belly and a more than passing irritation with his mother's grammatical mistakes.

From the boardinghouse, they moved to an apartment, which they furnished themselves: a solid maple bedroom suite and upholstered living room set were purchased on layaway from Sears. Maria gained enormous satisfaction from the regularity of her payments, and, a year and a half after the furniture's acquisition, from the final wad of bills, delivered in person to the customer accounts office downtown, which sealed ownership of these substantial possessions.

After the apartment, there came the house on Markham Street, a solid 1930s detached three-bedroom in a largely Portuguese neighborhood, with paneled halls and shiny brass fitments, which Maria kept as polished and perfect as if they were Mrs. Ellington's or Mrs. McDonald's.

Radek, by then Roddy, and ultimately Rod, grew up and away from his parents, a good student and a champion hockey player, popular with girls for his frayed blondish hair (his father's) and wide Slavic cheekbones (Maria's own). In the early sixties, he earned a scholarship to the University of Toronto to study engineering, and shortly after that he moved out of his tidy Markham Street room into student digs, along with four of his classmates, near Kensington Market: it was a sloppy, unkempt, ramshackle place with a sagging stoop and moldy carpets, which Maria could not visit without succumbing to the urge to clean, to make order, to Rod's frustration and ultimate fury. There came a day when, upon returning from the library to find his mother alone in the house mopping the buckled linoleum in the kitchen, Rod stormed: "For Christ's sake, Mom, can't you stop being a cleaning lady for even *ten* minutes? I wish you wouldn't come here at all, if that's how it's going to be!"—after which, in spite of his subsequent impassioned entreaties, Maria did not set foot inside any of Rod's homes until he married.

She couldn't, had she assessed the situation honestly, have truly approved of any woman that Radek might have loved: there was, for her and for Lev, too much at stake in the union of their son with any woman. But Lev, by nature quiet and noncommittal, did not rage as did Maria at Rod's engagement to Anita. Lev merely listened, his finger to his weather-baked and wearied cheek, his brow, long deprived of its towed fuzz, as bland and naked as a baby's. His lips retained their Polish pout, and Lev "phutted" them slightly as Maria ranted, but he did not part them far enough to speak. Maria had thought, she said, that they were rid of Anita, that she had been disposed of long ago: the old words, the Ukrainian words, for trollop and whore, slut, slattern, hoyden, minx, meretricious ne'er-do-well—these words she did not know in English and would not have spoken in front of Lev if she had, spewed inside her skull, in (how could she fail to recognize it, in spite of the long silence?) her own mother's voice.

Anita had been Rod's high school sweetheart, scrawny and unprepossessing then, her skirts too tight, her legs and arms like flailing sticks, her hair a thin mousy scraggle falling over her bony cheeks. Three years younger than Rod, she had stood mute in the Markham Street kitchen, a stain on her blouse, slovenly and sullen from the first, unable even to muster a

"Good afternoon, Mrs. Poniatowski," a courtesy which Maria had long come, in Canada, to expect, and of which Rod's male friends had shown themselves graciously capable.

The girl had then lived alone with her mother, a fat German frau (how could Maria approve of *that*? How could Lev countenance it?) and without apparent reference to a father. Whether he was dead or gone or had never existed was a mystery which would be glossed over till the end, and Maria, suspicious of the girl who clung so, cloying, unhealthy, to the strapping Rod, created for herself the story of Anita's disgraced mother's one-night stand, from which ghastly and anonymous coupling the dreg that was Anita had been spawned. But even then, when Rod was seventeen and Anita a too-precocious fourteen, with sex, or the desire of it, like a sickly nimbus about her, Maria had said no more to Lev than "She is not a nice girl," a hideous reduction, like the subtitles of a foreign film, of the complex of emotions and superstitions that whirled inside her.

Similarly, so many years later, when Rod announced his betrothal, in her attempt at fuming and railing Maria clenched her fists and reddened deeply but muttered only, to her husband, as she had originally, "She is not a nice girl, this Anita."

In between times, at university and afterwards, there had been others, or the rumor of others at least, and Maria, so certain that a chit of that sort would not serve for her glorious Canadian boy (not a whisper, not a memory in him of the camp where he had been born), could not be sure whether Anita had vanished, only like noxious flotsam to resurface, or whether, indeed, Maria in her obstinacy had simply willed a disappearance that had never taken place; whether in fact the

girl had been lurking all along, loitering mutely, a grasping suc-
cubus in the shadow of her boy.

Regardless, their engagement was a grave disappointment.
Maria had hoped for a daughter-in-law of good family, had fan-
tasized, indeed, that in the equalizing lecture halls and seminar
rooms of the university, Rod might meet a younger equivalent
of Judith Ellington or Leah Makerevich, a glossy-haired, well-
mannered patrician's daughter from the very gracious homes
where Maria had for so long been slaving. Failing that, a sturdy
peasant girl—from a farm near Hamilton, perhaps, or raised in
the orchards down by St. Catharines—would have sufficed, a
girl who knew, like Maria herself, how to be thrifty, how to
cook and sew, who would keep a clean house and want lots of
children: a girl, in short, who might have become a confidant,
even a friend.

But Anita? Where had she been in the intervening years,
while Rod had filled and strengthened into a plausible man of
business, his forearms thick, rosy and reassuring and the bully's
belly of his childhood returning, once the hockey playing
ceased, slowly but insistently, to swell the waistband of his
trousers? Anita had not left her mother's shabby house in the
neighborhood, an eyesore of peeling trim and greasy window-
panes in front of which pressed a snarl of nettles against a broken fence. She had not ventured to university but had, instead,
enrolled in beauty school, a lowly enough course but one
which even so she had lacked either the talent or the discipline
to complete. At the time of their engagement, Anita held a job
as the manicurist in a local salon, her own talons a tarty crimson and so long as to indicate that she did no housework at all.

Her once straggly hair was now frosted and bouffant, her googly eyes, a cold blue, were vigorously shadowed day and night with a glittering lavender paste and fronded by false lashes, and her skirts—it was the late sixties—though it hardly seemed possible, were still shorter and skimpier than they had formerly been.

And yet, in spite of this, in spite of these lowly and dismaying attributes, it was clear to Maria that Anita contrived, somehow, even at that early date, to look down upon her future in-laws. She made public, scornful announcement of the fact that neither Maria nor Lev could read or write English with ease; she told people that her fiancé's mother was a cleaning lady, even after Maria asked Rod to inform her that "housekeeper" was the more appropriate term; and, worst of all, she referred to Lev and Maria, within the latter's hearing, as "DPs," an appellation they had not suffered since soon after their arrival in Toronto and had come to consider an insult, not least, Maria pointed out to her son, because it had long ago ceased to be true: "We're not displaced," she said icily. "We are Canadian. Every bit as Canadian as that German mother of hers. We've been citizens now for fifteen years, and this is our home. Tell her," she insisted, "tell her that she is wrong. She cannot say this about us."

"But Mom," said Radek, pressing her arm, "she doesn't mean anything by it. It's true that's how you came here, right? There's no shame in that."

And Maria knew, because she heard Anita say it, again and again, that Radek had not scolded her, that he was entirely under her thumb.

When they married, in 1969, at the neighborhood Catholic church, Anita wore, to her mother-in-law's chagrin, a white satin minidress. The veil, which reached to her bony knees, was longer than her skirt, and she teetered down the aisle on her mother's meaty, mauve-encased arm, in three-inch sandals that bared her fuchsia-varnished toes. When Maria tried to explain the horror of this to Mrs. Ellington, herself by then widowed and alone in Laurel Heights, her own daughter married to one of that loathed species, the Americans, and removed to far-off California, the older woman merely peered from behind her thick cat's-eye glasses and sighed a condescending sigh: "At least they'll stay near home," she said. "Count yourself lucky on that score. And without any education, she won't run off and leave him. Cup of tea, Maria?"

Lev had seemed, to his own embittered wife (who, to her later shame, berated him for it), reconciled to the union, and to the loss it represented—of their aspirations, of their very son. "Who wins in the end, Lev?" asked Maria. "She's a German, isn't she? And we both know what that means." But in fact, as she reconstructed it later, he had been quietly heartbroken by Radek's choice. Who knew, in the end, what Lev had suffered in the war years before she met him? Not even Maria knew, although her nightmares gave rein to grim possibility; and just as she imagined so strongly a story behind Anita's birth that it lived in her mind as fact, she imagined, too, a story behind Lev's death.

The doctors might have called it lung cancer—and he a man who'd never smoked!—and they might well have blamed it on the years with Davidson's, on the rolls of asbestos Lev had bent over, and fiddled with, and, in minute, shredding particles, inhaled; but Maria knew that six weeks (it was, for poor Lev, merely six weeks between diagnosis and demise) was not the usual progress of such a disease: Mrs. Mallow had had her cancer three years before it was done. She located the source of his pallor, of his racking cough, of his deepening wrinkles and rasping breaths, of the reemergence of his ribs like a xylophone (how well she remembered the knock of those ribs, the knock of her own: what history they conjured!)—all this she knew was the resurfacing of a soul's grief, of a long-averted sickness unto death that had been held at bay by hope alone, hope for Radek and who he might have been, what he might have accomplished; hope dashed when Radek failed them both, married Anita, and allowed the Germans, thereby, to win at least one small corner—Lev's corner—of the war.

In her grief, this is what Maria told Mrs. Ellington, who again, as ever, peered at her expressionless and offered tea and suggested that she might need a holiday.

"I don't think it works quite like that, dear girl," said her employer, who still persisted in seeing Maria as a young woman barely twenty. "If the doctors say it's the asbestos, then they know what they're on about. Not that I would ever want to deny you your grief—I know, you remember, exactly what it's like. They were two fine men, Brice and Lev, but we have to learn to live without them. You can't live in the past, dear girl."

Maria stared incredulous that Mrs. Ellington should say such a thing to her, Maria, who knew it better than anyone; but Mrs. Ellington was oblivious to her outrage.

———

After Lev's death, Maria kept the house on Markham Street cleaner than it had ever been. She covered the living room furniture with bolts of thick clear plastic, and unfurled runners of ribbed, transparent vinyl across the rugs in the lines of her usual progress: from the front door to her armchair (Lev's, henceforth unoccupied, needed no protective pathway), to the television; and again from her armchair through the dining room to the kitchen. She preferred to sit and walk on plastic rather than to see her precious belongings deteriorate; and she imagined that Lev, always fastidious himself, watched her arrangements approvingly from on high. She forebore from using the overhead lights so as to preserve the bulbs as long as possible; and she sat, in winter, beneath blankets in front of the TV rather than raise the thermostat and risk straining the furnace. Radek, when he visited—which he did most often alone, without Anita, certainly in the years before the children were born—threw up his hands at her schemes: "You're crazy, Ma! You've got Dad's pension, and you're still working, and the house is all paid off, and you sit here in the cold and dark as if time had forgotten you—it's completely crazy!"

But in truth, Maria reveled in her domestic discretion. It delighted her to think that she passed through the house with as little disturbance as Lev's ghost. It was a complex satisfaction: that of not wasting, to be sure, the satisfaction bred into her in her parents' cabbage-scented cottage in faraway Gulyaypole; but also that of keeping safe, untainted, the life, the permanence, that she and Lev had built together over their Canadian years. She was aware, with all that had been suffered and had vanished, that these solid, tangible investments constituted her life entire, or what could be retained of it. The sofa, the bedroom suite, the coffee table that she polished so religiously (after long days spent polishing the tables of others) comprised a shrine, of a sort. They would—or should—outlast her. She did not like to consider that if, or rather when, she died, her son, and above all his wife, would tramp dismissively through the perfect rooms arranging only the sale, lock, stock and barrel, of their contents.

But even as Maria kept her home unchanging—a secret box, rarely visited, like a bank vault of her small treasures—she did not cease to live. It was in the early seventies, after Lev's death, that she took up dancing, for example. At last the single girl in search of amusement that she had not, back in '47 in Mrs. Makerevich's kitchen, been, she followed (she remembered!) the advice of her fellow servants there, and sought consolation in the ballroom of the Grand Palais down at the Lakeshore. Once a stylish hub, it was by then a slightly fusty gathering spot, its domed ceiling peeled and its bar dark; but still, on weekend evenings, it filled with men and women of her own age, chattery and excited as teenagers, eager to waltz and tango beneath the violet spotlights. Maria went first with an acquaintance from her church, also a widow, a stout Bulgarian with coiled plaits; but Mrs. Burov had not enjoyed herself, had found the heat and hubbub unseemly, while Maria, wiry still and, with the help of a little Clairol, raven-haired, had been enchanted. Gliding over the glossy floor in flat-soled slippers, her skirt billowing, she had felt the bloom of youth returning to her cheeks, and had caught herself giggling behind her hand and smiling sidelong when a swarthy Spaniard, easily sixty, complimented her graceful footwork.

She returned thereafter without Mrs. Burov, found herself primping and painting her lips in anticipation of her outings. She loved, especially, the luxury of a taxicab which she allowed herself for the rides home, the steps from the steamy heat of the dance hall into the cold wind off the lake, when the sweat of her pirouettes and gliding turned chill inside her dress, and the awaiting car door opened to welcome her, warm again, and shuttle her in delicious silence across town. She pressed her nose almost to the window for those rides, and ogled the city lights and youthful crowds that filled the streets as if watching, all wonder, a glorious film; and carried in her head, as its jaunty soundtrack, the live band at the Grand Palais, to whose gay rhythms she had so lately swayed.

Back in Markham Street on dancing nights, she prepared a ritual cup of tea, humming the dance melodies in the kitchen fluorescence, and sometimes, just sometimes, in cheerful abandon, she would allow her cup and saucer to remain dirty in the sink overnight—not so much out of idleness (what was one more dish to wash?) but for the relived pleasure, upon discovery in the morning of the lipstick-traced china, of the previous evening's girlish release.

It was after Lev's death, too, that Maria granted herself, upon Mrs. Ellington's advice, her first real holiday. Her initial foray was to Florida, in March, where she took a service apartment in a tower in Fort Myers and strolled, for the first time in her life, along the burning sand of a tropical beach. The following year, however, with her ever-frugal eye, she opted for a package deal to Cuba, and was thenceforth converted. That it was a Communist stronghold, like her childhood home, barely crossed her mind: she loved the faded grandeur of Havana, the mixture of glitz and reassuring poverty (the Cubans, like herself, wore their clothes threadbare and resoled their shoes until the tops fell away in tatters: it seemed, to Maria, only a sign of good sense). She loved, too, so she discovered, the great heat, and the near-sombreness of siesta hour, when all retreated from the unflinching glare to shuttered quiet, only to emerge, as shadows lengthened, with renewed freshness and vigor. She loved the scrabbling roosters, crowing in yards and vacant lots, their claws plucking at the rubble. She loved, above all, the Latin music: in Cuba, in her modest hotel, she danced every night, often till one or two in the morning. She never felt old, and noted with pleasure that many people of her age stayed later, even, than she. She was partial to the food, and the smells of burning—even of garbage, sweetish and strong—that the hot breezes carried. She admired the skins of the Cubans, the rich palette of whites, yellows, olives and browns, in which her own dark coloring seemed to meld and allow her to pass for a native. She learned a few words of Spanish.

Men—younger men, in their forties or late thirties—with curls and sharp teeth, in loose shirts and pressed trousers, spun Maria on the dance floors of the new hotel, or on the promenade by the shore, in the briny sea air that settled after dusk, their deft steps illuminated by the strings of multicolored bulbs that draped the outlines of the dance floor. Maria, rippling, admiring her own brown biceps, felt the thud of the drums in her belly and in the soles of her feet. She knew, or at least she surmised, that these partners offered more than their sweating palms and their swift, urgent smiles; but she had no more interest in gigolos than in the quantities of embroidered straw hats and kitschy T-shirts on sale in the beachside stalls, and so she pretended not to know, merely shook her head and laughed.

Sometimes, at dawn, behind the louvered shutters of her hotel room, listening to the lazy whir of the overhead fan and the shush of the sea on the sand, Maria wondered at the distance she had traveled, from the cold ditch beneath the hedgerow. But her amazement was fleeting: she did not have the temperament to dwell, but rather the impulse to movement like a coiled spring in her torso, and she would, on such mornings, fling back the damp sheet and dress in the gloom, padding out to walk the sand's length by the light of the rising sun, to hear the birds and feel the day's heat rising to settle like a moist skin upon her skin. Alone, on these walks, she occasionally sighted seabirds, dive-bombing pelicans with their jiggling gorges, or the jittering, graceful herons, all angles, that stalked the shallows at the bay's deserted end. Breakfasting with her fellow Canadians upon her return—sampling papaya and mango for the first time, or showering her cereal with the rich white full-fat milk she never consumed at home—Maria never spoke of the dawn, or the birds: she considered them private, hers, a gift. A recompense, somehow, although she could not have said for what. She chatted instead about the dance music, or told stories about her son, her grandchildren, some of them invented, all of them breathless, delivered with giggles that set her gold earrings aquiver.

Rod approved of his mother's Caribbean holidays, although Anita, like Mrs. Ellington, raised an eyebrow at the mention of

Cuba and said only, "Isn't it Communist? Doesn't that scare you?" Every year, once the children were born, Maria brought back small gifts for Kelly and Paul: tiny T-shirts, bead bracelets, coconut rattles; although she suspected that Anita only threw them away.

Rod, in that decade, grew successful. His brusque, solid manner inspired confidence; he was good at his job. By 1983, when Kelly was four and Paul a plump, jolly two-year-old who resembled the infant Radek in all aspects, Rod and Anita were able to move their perfect Canadian family to Oakville. Rod chose a split-level ranch house within walking distance of the GO Train, and claimed that his commute to the office, near Toronto's City Hall, was no longer than it had been from the West End. They had an open-plan living room with exposed beams and a patio for barbecuing; Rod chose the giant maple at the back of their sprawling lot in which he would build a tree house for the kids when they were old enough. The house had as many bathrooms as bedrooms—four—and as soon as little Paul was old enough for nursery school, Anita took a job as the receptionist for a small manufacturer of tachometers whose plant was ten minutes' drive from the house. When Maria expressed her surprise at this decision, Anita revealed that her mother—the hated German trollop—was to move into their fourth bedroom to help take care of the children.

Bloated and prematurely crippled by arthritis, Anita's mother couldn't keep up her own home ("as if she ever had," complained Maria to Mrs. Ellington, who sighed and blinked behind her ever more owlish spectacles. "She lives in a pigsty"), and Rod had agreed to take in his mother-in-law in return for her services as a nanny.

Maria, who had not felt especially welcome in Oakville from the first, saw this maneuver as a terrible betrayal. She did not speak to her son about it, and she did not blame *him* (he had always, she knew, been under the thumb of his harpie-wife), but she waited, and waited, to be invited to spend time with her family, and vented her spleen at their silence to Mrs. Ellington.

Mrs. Ellington, sharp-tongued herself, listened—albeit not with infinite patience—and strove to drown her housekeeper's sorrows in endless cups of tea. "I think you should *ask* to visit, Maria," she volunteered at last. "They can't refuse you. You're the children's grandmother, after all. You have every bit as much right as that other woman."

"It's Anita, Mrs. Ellington." Maria shook her head for the umpteenth time, folding her paper napkin into ever smaller squares and allowing the tears to well up in her eyes. "She is not a good girl. I told Radek right from the start."

"Nobody likes their in-laws, Maria." Mrs. Ellington lifted her chin and sniffed like a hound at the breeze from the apartment's open window (she was, by now, no longer on Laurel Heights: going blind and alone, she had fitted her life into the modern, square confines of the Manley Avenue flat). "Or very few do. It's a type of affection as rare as hen's teeth."

Maria looked blank.

"Hens have no teeth, don't you see? It's an expression. Just an expression. My point is—look at Judith's husband, the nasty American flag-waving goat. I couldn't like him if he were the last man on earth. But I'm not going to let that stop me seeing Judith, or the kids. It's beside the point."

"But Mrs. Ellington," said Maria, "Anita runs him, she runs the house. She looks down on me. She thinks I'm stupid because my English is not so good."

"Nonsense. Your English is excellent."

"Not for writing and reading, Mrs. Ellington. You know that."

"She's a high school dropout, Maria."

"I know."

"She's not worthy of your boy, let alone you. You just have to keep in mind that she's not worthy."

Maria briefly contemplated the notion of worthiness. "But what am I supposed to do, Mrs. Ellington? She doesn't invite me to the house."

"Invite them to yours, then. Invite them to Markham Street."

Maria took her employer's advice. But she found that her invitations were frequently rebuffed: Anita found it was too far, or too complicated to arrange, or her own mother was too unwell, or the children were too restless, or too tired. It happened more than once that Radek would promise a family visit, for a Saturday, say, only to ring in the morning to announce that he was coming on his own: Kelly had ballet class, or soccer practice; or Paul had been sick in the night. Maria chose to believe the excuses, as her pride demanded; but when she walked out to Lev's grave on Sunday after mass, as she did, rain or shine, in all but the most bitter winter weather, she knelt by her husband's tomb and whispered vituperation against her daughter-in-law—quietly, always, so that the neighboring spirits would not be unsettled by her ranting, but purposefully, forcefully, from a seemingly bottomless well of ill will.

"You were right, Lev, to shut your eyes to this," she told the cold stone, as she arranged her small bouquet (culled from the garden or purchased from the Korean greengrocer, depending on the season) in the jam jar that stood in front of it. "This Anita is so wicked. I *spoke* to Kelly, and I could tell that she wanted to come: 'I miss you grandma,' she said to me. And the little boy, Paul! He's his father all over again, he is Radek exactly, sometimes serious, sometimes laughing. He doesn't speak on the telephone very much. I don't mean anything to him. Not yet. It's not Radek's fault, you know. It's that Anita. She's getting fat now, Lev, just like I knew she would. She's not pretty, and she doesn't take care, and she'll go like her mother, round as a potato, you wait and see. She's eating all McDonald's, says she doesn't like to cook, but that can't be good for the kids, nah? I offer cooking, but she don't want it. That mother, living with them, she's a bad one, worse. You remember her, at the wedding, all fat and purple? Hmm?"

Lev kept his counsel, but Maria drew comfort from the mere fact of his proximity. At his grave, on a rise above the Humber River just before it opened into Lake Ontario, in a field of tombstones set out in shaded alleys and lit by the water and the sky, Maria felt consoled. She knew each season, and each moment of each season, in that place, the distant road sounds and nearby birdsongs, the changing tint of the foliage. She knew the names of all the dead around Lev, as if they were his colleagues or his classmates, and some of the neglected graves she swept and tidied in discreet homage to all who must know her husband.

When Radek did bring his family to Markham Street, the visits were strained and formal. Kelly and Paul perched on the plastic-covered chesterfield in their best outfits and fidgeted irritably, staring at the wall of family photos—which included pictures of themselves at every age—or at the blank television screen. Anita and Rod hovered, somehow too large for the sitting room, their very clothes seemingly tight and ill-fitting. Maria, made nervous, heard herself squawking and loathed herself. She cooked elaborate lunches—stews and casseroles, vast bowls of boiled vegetables, fruitcakes and puddings—which her guests only picked at (even Radek, a hearty man; and even his wife, whose girth was spreading, year by year, to outstrip her husband's) and never complimented. After lunch, while the adults had tea (Anita always asked for coffee, and somehow, she didn't know why, Maria never had any to hand), the children were invariably set loose in the back garden, where they trampled Maria's rows of vegetables, her tidy flower beds, and from which—she never mentioned it, except to Lev and Mrs. Ellington—they trailed clods of mud into the kitchen, small, stubborn tracks that sometimes found their way beyond the linoleum, off the plastic runners, into the fibres of the pristine cream broadloom. By three or three-thirty, Anita would be mumbling about her mother alone at home, or about the distance they had to drive, and as if in concert, the four of them would regroup and drift towards the door, waving away the foil-wrapped remainder of the cake, or the leftover stew in its Tupperware bowl. In spite of all her harbored hopes for these visits, Maria could feel nothing but relief when they were over, and would spend the remaining hours before she went out dancing in furious cleaning of the smears and disorder her family had wrought. On the nights after these rare invasions, Maria danced at the Grand Palais with particular abandon, almost with desperation, and once even allowed a wrinkled suitor to kiss her cheek. (He then asked for her telephone number, but that, even in extremis, Maria had no intention of divulging.)

In 1989, when Kelly was ten and Paul eight, Anita's mother died of a heart attack. Maria attended the funeral, out in Oakville: the service took place in a plush, sombre chapel of rest where the German lay stony and immense in her open coffin. There were few mourners. Maria was dismayed to see the desolation in her grandchildren's faces, their skin pale as the dirty snow outside— it was late November—and their eyes red and swollen with crying. She wondered whether Kelly and Paul would manifest such sorrow if she herself were to die. When her own turn came to pay her respects to the dead, she leaned over the corpse and longed to touch it, but satisfied herself with sniffing, for the ugly smells of death or of embalming fluid. She couldn't smell a thing. Even now, the old woman was, she thought, wearing far too much makeup, and her paisley dress was bunched unbecomingly at the armpits. For once, however, her fingernails were clean. Maria noticed that the coffin, brass-handled, was lined with white satin: no expense had been spared. Would they extend themselves thus for her own funeral? She wasn't at all sure.

The following spring, as if to assert their freedom, Radek and Anita bought a summer cottage in Muskoka, and a motorboat. To Maria's surprise, they invited her to spend a fortnight with them there, in June.

"I don't know, Mrs. Ellington," she said to her now frail employer who, almost the age of the century, was practically a nonagenarian. "What do you think? Maybe they don't really want me to say yes? Maybe they're hoping I'll say no, because that Anita, you know, when we're together, it's difficult. Two weeks is a long time, nah?"

"Don't be ridiculous, Maria," replied Mrs. Ellington above the din of a Gilbert and Sullivan operetta, in time to which she persisted in tapping her foot despite the gravity of the discussion. "All these years you've said they don't pay you enough attention, and now they offer and you think of saying no? Muskoka's beautiful. You'll have a lovely time. And if you don't like it, you can always catch the first bus home."

Maria thought of the Greyhound from Sudbury, all those years before, leaving the lumber camp at Tagomack with Lev by her side and Radek on her lap, headed towards Toronto which was not yet then "home," which was pure possibility. "I suppose you're right," she said. "I know how to take the bus, at least."

In mid-June, then, in the back seat of Radek's silver LeSabre, with the tatted back of Anita's frosted head between her and the road in front, with Paul, almost nine, nestled amiably against her thigh while Kelly bobbed beside him to the muted throb of her Walkman, Maria retraced the route towards her first Canadian residence. Nothing along the way looked especially familiar. More than forty years had passed, after all. But Maria found her stomach bolting and her heart enlarging nevertheless: there had to be some meaning in this return.

In fact, Radek and Anita's cottage was many miles from Tagomack, on Lake of Bays. The flora—the pine trees and maples, the moss on the lakeshore boulders—was as Maria remembered, as were the swarms of black flies and the crystalline water, but she could not find Tagomack in the cozy comforts of the modern cottage, with its pale blue aluminum siding and inground septic tank. Rod and Anita had furnished the place in a single, mammoth sweep through Ikea, so that all the rooms were decorated in light wood and bright colors, and smelled faintly of the chemicals with which the upholstery had been treated, a synthetic, new-car smell.

Maria was installed in the smallest of the three bedrooms, a cubby beside the kitchen with a view, behind the rickrack curtains, onto the hood of the Buick and towards the dirt road beyond. Her bed was narrow, and too firm for Maria's taste, and the chest of drawers, of white particle board with plastic handles, seemed to her too flimsy to use. She put her suitcase under the bed, with all her clothes still in it, and resolved to iron each item anew as she removed it for wearing (only to discover—she ought to have known—that Anita had no iron).

Maria began to realize that, just as she did not quite know how to arrange her wardrobe in her little room, she did not know how to fit herself into the rhythms of her son and his family. They had their own habits and ways of speaking—little Kelly was, Maria thought, intolerably insolent and offhand with her father, a breach of etiquette that Anita appeared tacitly to condone—and their own, unquestioning order for the unfolding of meals, a harum-scarum free-for-all that never seemed to involve a proper *course*, and only rarely required cutlery. They had their patterns for squabbling, for planning, for moving about singly or as a group, in all of which she hovered on the periphery, an afterthought. She had never had to adapt in quite this manner before, although adaptation had been, in her youth, not merely her forte but her survival. She was accustomed to accommodation into the lives of families only as a housekeeper—for the Ellingtons or the McDonalds or the Pollocks—and so, in the cottage, reverted to these known paths. She found tasks for herself without asking: she washed the windows inside and out while Rod, Anita and the kids went swimming; she crept into the kitchen before dawn and emptied all the cupboards to scrub the shelves clean, and then carefully rewashed every cup and dish and pot, all of which seemed to her filmed with stickiness and grease. She spent an afternoon weeding what had once been a flower bed along the side of the cottage, where a few stubborn nasturtiums and sweet peas still pushed; and she trimmed the wild lilac bush with a kitchen knife because Rod had no shears.

All this Anita suffered with silent, ominous disapproval, her chin trembling with barely perceptible rage when she shuffled into the kitchen in her furry purple housecoat to find it undone, or when, wrapped in a huge, leopard-spotted towel, she picked her way back up from the dock to discover her mother-in-law, damp rag in hand, sudsing the picture window onto the lake from the perch of the brand-new Ikea stepladder. But when Maria, mop, bucket and rags in hand, decided to tackle the boathouse ("So many spiders, yeah? Filthy!" she exclaimed with her girlish giggle, and her nose wrinkled in a simian grin), Anita could keep quiet no longer.

"We can *afford* a cleaning lady, you know," she said, with a smile that, intended to mask her irritation, succeeded only in sharpening her disdain. "We didn't invite you up here to spend all day, every day, creeping around behind us with a scrubbing brush!"

Maria's face opened, then closed. She put down her bucket, her mop.

"Don't be like that, Mom," said Rod in a wheedling tone. "All Anita means is that we want you to have a holiday. You know, to take a rest. You shouldn't be *working*. That's all."

Maria's hands hung at her sides. She lifted her chin as if to speak, but said nothing.

"Besides, Mom, you know that boathouses are meant to be dirty—they're like garages, except on water. Heck, you want the spiders to have *somewhere* to live, don't you?"

"Yuck," Paul chimed in. "I don't. I want Grandma to kill them all."

"Well," said Anita, "I believe in live and let live, and your grandmother can kill all the spiders she wants to at her house, but *here*—"

"I'm going to put the mop away," Maria murmured. When she had done, she retreated to her little room and lay on her bed with her shoes on (although she rested her heels over its foot so as not to soil the spread with her soles), staring at the ceiling. She was too angry even to think, and although she heard Paul's tremolo asking his mother whether Grandma wouldn't like to

come swimming, and heard Anita answer, in the voice made
more resonant by her recent swollen size, that maybe Grandma
was too tired just now ("Tired? Too tired?" Maria's inner voice
spat contemptuously), she did not move a muscle. She watched
a fly buzz around the walls. She heard the clatter of the family
gathering their gear—fins and a mask for Paul, glossy magazines and a romance novel for Anita, the supermarket sort with
gilded covers (Maria knew it, saw it in her mind's eye), Kelly's
ubiquitous yellow Walkman—and the tramp of their feet on
the steps, and the rippling thud as the last, probably Rod,
slammed the front door. She lay there still, in the quiet, aware
of the caterpillar ridges of the chenille bedspread beneath her
arms and legs, aware of the play of sunlight in the pines outside
the window, aware of the fly's grinding buzz as it stopped and
started; paralyzed by her fury, Maria lay in wait. She could
catch the bus; she would not catch the bus. She had nine more
days to endure.

Shortly after noon, Paul and Kelly came together to her door.
They knocked gently before opening, but did not wait for her
to answer. They stood at the foot of the bed, their tangled hair
wet, their T-shirts damp with the imprint of their bathing suits,
their skin fresh and freckled from their morning in the water.

"Will you get up now, Grandma?" Paul whispered, as if afraid
to break the churchly silence. "We're going to have lunch."

Maria peered at her grandchildren without raising her head
from the pillow.

"Dad's gone into town to get sandwiches," offered Kelly.

"Submarine sandwiches. And doughnuts from Tim Horton's. Please get up, Grandma."

Paul lunged forward and pressed his warm nose into her neck. "Please don't be sick, Grandma, *please?*"

"Sick?" said Maria, struggling all of a sudden to sit up. "Who's sick?"

"Mom said you were sick."

"Grandma's not sick, Paulie." Maria wondered what her daughter-in-law intended, in lying to the children. "Grandma's never sick. Strong as a horse."

Kelly giggled.

"What?"

"Say it again, Grandma," said Kelly, still smirking. Maria noticed the buds of the girl's breasts, two small points against her shirt. "Your accent's so funny."

"You're making fun of Grandma now?" Maria laughed to hide her hurt. "Maybe that makes Grandma sick!"

"Never!" cried Paul, who had retreated far enough to allow her to stand, but who hovered still, waiting to throw his arms around her waist. "You're strong as a horse, Grandma! You just said!"

In this way, the crisis passed. In the afternoon, following the meal, eaten by Rod standing, at which Maria yearned for Mrs. Ellington's crustless white bread and her cut-glass bowl of Bick's yum-yum pickles, and watched aghast as Anita, with grotesque daintiness, downed an entire mixed-meats sub and three glazed crullers, along with a bottle of Carlsberg for which she did not bother with a glass—following this, the family gathered their belongings to go for a ride in the motorboat. Rod donned a blue baseball cap with his company's logo embroidered on it; Anita layered her fair skin with greasy suntan cream; and the children bickered over whether to bring cookies or doughnuts, Coca-Cola or 7-Up, in the iced cooler. Even Maria put on her cotton sunhat with the floppy brim, which she usually saved for Cuba, and which carried about it the whiff of mothballs from the Markham Street trunk in which it was habitually stored.

It wasn't, as Maria told Mrs. Ellington later, that she didn't *enjoy* the boat ride: the pulse of the engine and the buffeting wavelets, the puffy white leatherette banquette on which she sat between her grandchildren, drinking in the breeze. She enjoyed, too, the dense trees along the shore, thick like the earth's pelt, and the glimpse of chalets and cabins among their branches. She enjoyed being hot and cold at once, hot from the sun and cold from the wind, and she enjoyed the flat, foam-tipped swath of wake the boat left behind. She took pleasure in the water's solemn clarity, its visible depths, and the sheen of the light upon it from a distance. She liked, too, the flicker and snap of the small Canadian flag at the stern, behind her head, and the sight of other craft—two canoes and a kayak, a little sailboat and three or four other boats, smaller than Rod's, with outboard motors that churned the glassy lake and emitted roaring, close diesel fumes. She enjoyed all of this; she just didn't see the point of it. She was not a person to act without motivation, and her purpose on the water wasn't clear to her. When, in the middle of the lake, Rod turned off the engine and began to fiddle with his fishing rod and a new-looking coffee can in which Paul had gathered worms for his father, Maria realized that only she was surprised: Paul and Kelly peeled off their T-shirts and slipped over the boat's side into the water to swim in circles behind the boat, while Rod settled himself up at the bow, beyond the spattered windscreen, and cast his line. Anita, with a sigh, huddled in the modest shade of the captain's seat with a Carlsberg propped between her thighs, and pulled her paperback out of her beach bag.

"Not going to swim?" she asked her mother-in-law, one eye closed against the glare.

Maria, never a strong swimmer—never, in truth, a swimmer at all: she waded in the Caribbean, but never relinquished her footing (because where, in Gulyaypole, in Germany, in the cold months at Tagomack and the busyness of real life that so swiftly succeeded them, would Maria have ever learned to swim?)—did not want to reveal as much to Anita. She could hear Anita's whining voice deriding her to Radek: "She can't read or write, and she can't even swim? What can the old bat do, besides clean houses?"

"It's too cold for me," she said simply, and folded her hands in her lap.

"Only the Caribbean will do, eh? You've been spoiled!"

"No, no. Just too cold today."

But short of swimming, there was little to entertain Maria for the hour or more that they drifted at the heart of the lake. Rod, his back turned to his family, sat immobile and apparently content, his rod angled slightly upwards and its line, not quite taut, arcing outwards to the water. Anita waved at flies and turned the pulpy pages of her novel, looking up from time to time to sight her children's sleek wet heads, and then swigging, almost aggressively, as if in defiance, from her beer bottle. Paul and Kelly frolicked like porpoises, in the tireless way of children, occasionally resting at the ladder on the side of the boat and then splashing off again, turning somersaults or tackling each other underwater.

Maria could not have explained to Mrs. Ellington the helplessness she felt in that hour, the hideous superfluity. It wasn't the morning's rage; it was instead an agony, a physical agitation, a more profound sense of not belonging than she had ever before, in all her life, experienced. She was to this scene like the flag on the back of the boat, or like the occasional burst of an engine in the distance: a tiny, rootless fact, an irrelevance. She followed the line of trees at the horizon and the pale cumulus stretch above, felt the gentle chuck-sucking of the water at the boat's underside, and for the first time she could recall, she asked herself, "How did I get here? What am I doing here? Why is this so?"

She watched Anita reading, and could not tell whether Anita was truly oblivious to her gaze, or concentrating all the harder on her novel to avoid it. She watched the children, waited—it seemed so long a wait!—for them to notice her; smiled, and waved. She did not know that when she smiled her silver teeth caught the sun and glittered, visible to them far off in the water.

She grew cold, in spite of the light, but she did not move around in the boat. She imagined falling over the side, if she were to move, her flowered skirt billowing up around her neck, her sandals weighing her down, dragging her farther into the lake's sombre depths. She imagined gasping for air and swallowing the lake instead, icy gulps of the greening, blueing, ever deeper water as it closed coldly over her skull. Would they save her? Would they try? Anita might go so far as to put down her novel, to move her beer bottle from between her legs; she might shade her eyes with a fleshy, pale hand and watch the gurgly eddy into which Maria had vanished. But she would not speak, or come rushing. And how would Radek know, with his back turned; and even if he knew, what would it mean to him? Only the children—and in truth, only Paul. But for all his frantic diving, his spindly arms would be too weak, his flailing ineffectual. At best, he might salvage a hank of hair, or the gold chain snapped from about her neck.

All this, Maria lived through in the placid hour. She felt the pit of mourning in her stomach: only she would mourn herself. She and Mrs. Ellington, who needed her. Even Jack Mc-Donald and his wife—although they would attend the funeral, to be sure—would be only passingly sad. She was old to them, after all, of the generation whose turn it was to die, one way or another, sooner or later. The buffer against their own mortality. Only for Mrs. Ellington was she still the vibrant, unlined Maria Poniatowski, of the dark cloud of hair and the easy laugh, with the handsome young husband and bonny little boy, the young woman whose early trials (of those Mrs. Ellington knew at least a little, knew enough), whose losses, could still be subsumed in the real joy of new life. Nobody else alive could see her now as she had once been, the way a lover sees, with the intimate knowledge of the intervening years between there and here, a knowledge that in its rhythmed quotidian insistence fairly obliterated those years, rendered them invisible. Were Olga to see Maria now, for example, Maria knew she would see foremost the lost years, the ravaging. Not so with Mrs. Ellington. It did not matter, or not so much, that Mrs. Ellington was all but blind; she could still see Maria clearly, as Maria wanted to be seen. It did not occur to Maria then to wonder whether it mattered that Mrs. Ellington was her employer, before she was a friend, or kin.

But less than a year later, when things with Mrs. Ellington—or rather, with her humor; because not with her health—had gone from bad to worse, when Mrs. Ellington, minute, imperious and unhinged, berated and dismissed Maria in the living room on Manley Avenue, Maria was forced to wonder what it was, for decades, that had passed between them, and whether, in the end, it was above all a matter of the tidy envelope of bills that Mrs. Ellington placed discreetly on the front hall table before lunchtime every Tuesday. Because if it had been more than that, how could she have behaved as she had done?

It had been building for months. Maybe it was Mrs. Ellington's new blood pressure medication that was behind the souring of her temper; or perhaps the doctor's insistence that, on account of her blood sugar levels, she renounce all manner of sweets, her beloved Fig Newtons included. (She still bought them, and laid them out on a saucer for Maria; so maybe it was that: the mounting resentment of seeing Maria eat what she was herself denied?) Or perhaps it was the acceleration of her blindness, so that, by '91, she could no longer decipher, letter by painstaking letter, the headlines of the newspaper, even with her special little telescope. And it may just have been her rage at obsolescence, at the creeping approach of death which, once past ninety, Mrs. Ellington could no longer ignore: if that was the case, then her insistence on Maria's youthful vigor was surely part of the problem.

Because in the months before the explosion—an explosion about sandwiches and furniture wax—Mrs. Ellington grew snide and bitter not about Maria's failings, but about her qualities. "Regular as bloody clockwork," she would snarl, when Maria opened the front door at five minutes to eight. "I guess there's no rest for the wicked." And she grumbled about the half-and-half for Maria's coffee, although Maria had drunk her coffee thus since 1947. She didn't want Maria to clean around her feet, she said, by which she seemed to mean that she didn't want to be in the room where Maria was working; and yet, by that time, Mrs. Ellington didn't go out very much, so what was Maria to do? She rebuked Maria one week for turning on the vacuum cleaner when she was listening to a book on tape, then castigated her the next for running the kitchen taps during the radio's hourly news report. She seemed, that spring, to bristle and grimace at almost everything Maria said, whether Maria made conversation about her trip to Cuba, or talked about Rod, Anita and the kids, or whether she stuck to matters of business, like the obstinate grease stains on Mrs. Ellington's best silk blouse or the fact that there was a tear in one of the pillowcases or—and this was the source of the decisive out-burst—the mere need for more wax with which to polish the rarely used dining room suite.

"Get me this, get me that! We're out of wax, Mrs. Elling-ton! We need more laundry soap, Mrs. Ellington! You're in my hair, week after damn week, and at my age, haven't I had about enough of it? Always so cheerful, pretending to make my life easier, but you're a bloody pain in the neck is what you are," Mrs. Ellington yelled. "If it's not one thing it's another, and I'm running around after you the whole damn time, making sure there's cream for your coffee, or white bread for your sand-wiches. And will you eat anything that would make my life simpler? You don't like tuna, you won't touch shrimp salad, in fact, you won't touch *anything* that comes out of a can, so I have to rush off to find you ham, or salami, or that fatty kielbasa—but make sure it's not turkey, Mrs. Ellington! As if it were easy! As if I could just hop up to the deli like someone half my age! And you won't eat soup, or leftovers, and you've got to have your stupid pickles just so, and I cut off your crusts for you as though you were a child of five, even though I'm blind as a god-damned bat and likely to cut my own fingers off in the bargain! Well, I'll tell you something, Maria, I've had it up to here"—Mrs. Ellington raised her arm above her head and thrashed at the air—"and I can get along just as well without your help, thank you very much. I don't need this aggravation any longer. It's less work for me to throw a few clothes in the washing ma-chine and wipe the table with a damp cloth than it is for me to have to put up with *this*, week after infernal week! Not to men-tion your *incessant* talking!"

Mrs. Ellington, veritably purple, stopped and huffed for air. Her entire wizened body was aquiver, as if plugged into a socket. Her hair seemed to stand on end. Maria, dumbstruck, gaped.

"Do you not hear what I'm saying, Maria Poniatowski? I don't want your help. You aren't needed anymore. Do you understand English? I'm telling you to get out. Your money's on the table, it's ready and waiting, as ever. I made a special trip to the bank yesterday—of course I did. So just take it, and *get out*!" This last exhortation was high and prolonged, a mourner's bottomless wail. Maria did not wait for more.

You would not have thought such a rupture could be repaired. Maria did not, for one, think that it would be possible; not, that is, after she hurried home from the site of the drama to await the phone call from Mrs. Ellington offering abject apology, and asking her in heartfelt contrition why she had not, at the very least, taken the envelope of money, and inviting her, perhaps, to come for supper by way of making up, so that then, the way a severed fingertip can be salvaged if it is sewn immediately on again, they might have resumed their Tuesday rituals as if nothing untoward had happened. But Maria waited, in her armchair, as the afternoon light softened and dusk fell, and then she waited in the dark, without stirring, willing Mrs. Ellington to act; and yet, when the telephone rang around eight it was only Radek, her son, in his peremptory biweekly communication, and not Mrs. Ellington at all.

Maria did not, that day, and not for many days thereafter, have the courage to tell Rod what had happened. Similarly, she would later discover, it was two and half weeks before Mrs.

Ellington—who spoke to her daughter every evening—finally revealed to Judith the unfortunate state of affairs. At that point, Judith told Maria once it was all over, when Judith jumped on the next plane from California and arrived at her mother's door, she discovered that the old woman was camping in increasing squalor, her clothes dirty, her cutlery and china sticky, and her kitchen floor grainy and streaked underfoot. But Mrs. Ellington was unrelenting still, in those early days of separation, and would not permit Judith even to telephone Maria, so that she did so on the sly from a pay phone in the subway station with the intermittent whooshing roar of the TTC trains eating her apologies.

To say that Maria was shocked by Mrs. Ellington's behavior could not begin to explain her sentiments. She was not undone: Maria was not of a constitution to be undone, after all that she had endured, and she made fruitful use of her newly free Tuesdays, with only a faint burst of surprise, each week, when she awoke at her usual hour only to recall that she was no longer awaited. But she felt hardened by the estrangement, coming as it did apparently from nowhere, and it resolved her the more firmly to protect and preserve the fabric of her Markham Street house: in the end, this was all that she could rely on, the furniture and fittings, the solidity of her paneled hallways and the trim, budding rows of tomatoes and zucchinis in her yard. Mrs. Ellington, whom she had held to be the stable and benevolent repository of as much of her life as anyone, had proven, like an animal suddenly ferocious, ultimately alien. Most hurtful, perhaps, was her parting gibe about the cash— that, of the rant, was what Maria replayed most often in her mind—as if the decades of devotion she had shown the old woman were to be reduced to a pile of worn bills, as if money had any bearing on what the two of them had shared.

"I don't know, Judith," Maria said over tea (Mrs. Ellington's brand—Red Rose—to which Maria had long ago converted) when Judith came to Markham Street to try to effect a reunion. "Your mother, she's changed. Maybe she's sick, maybe it's just getting old, but I didn't know she could be so nasty. She was nasty to me, Judith. About working, about talking, about money, even. It's like she's crazy. I don't think I could take no more."

"She didn't mean it, Maria. She didn't know what she was saying—"

"She said it, nah? So she musta been thinking it."

"No, no, Maria. She was—it was like she was having a fit, you know? You remember when I was a girl, the things she sometimes said to me?"

"I sure do, Judith. I remember—" Maria laughed through her veil of tears. "You two would fight something awful. One time she pulled your hair. Oh boy, you did scream then. I remember."

"She's always had a sharp tongue. It gets away with her. But she doesn't mean it."

"Maybe. I don't know, Judith, still—"

This was when Judith explained that Mrs. Ellington was utterly lost without Maria, that she couldn't possibly go on in Manley Avenue on her own. Judith said that Mrs. Ellington had mistakenly put bleach in the washing machine thinking it was soap, and had ruined a whole batch of towels. "We can't imagine what it's like to go blind like that, Maria. She's so proud, and it's such a terrible frustration. It's as if all the lights were going out, one by one, and she were being left completely in the dark. It's awful."

This struck a chord with Maria. It was not the same, but it was similar, to what she felt herself, which was, too, a sensation of the lights going out—of the people who could know her, or who cared to know her, disappearing—until, rather than not seeing, Maria was above all unseen. And if she were unseen, unknown, as she had felt on the boat in the middle of Lake of Bays, how then could she be sure that she *was* at all, that she breathed and signified still, that she carried inside her all the irreconcilable experiences, the long, woven filament of life that stretched back through the years and across the continents? In their different ways, Maria realized, both she and Mrs. Ellington were becoming invisible. And perhaps, then, she decided, although not without a grim sense of resignation, they were doomed to each other, perhaps that was the truth: bound, in spite of themselves, to illuminate one another and to help each other to cast some semblance of a shadow.

Which was why, after six months' hiatus, and after Mrs. Ellington's brittle but apparently genuine apology, Maria agreed, without rancor, to return to Manley Avenue. They took up their routines ("Cup of tea, Maria?") as if nothing had happened, and they only rarely, glancingly, touched upon the months of their separation. When Maria went back, there was, too, the thrill of a challenge: Judith's occasional visits and her attempts to make order had not stanched the apartment's entropic slide. There was more work to be done than there had been in years, and Maria derived a certain satisfaction from the warm burning in her arms and legs, from the dull lumbar ache that ensued, Tuesday nights, for over a month.

"It keeps me in shape," she told Mrs. Ellington as she scrubbed the bathtub on her knees. "It's good for dancing, nah? Don't want to get old!"

"You're not old, Maria! You're a spring chicken," said Mrs. Ellington with a sigh.

"I'm an old-age pensioner, Mrs. Ellington. I'm an old grandma, just like you. The kids are big now, growing up."

Kelly and Paul were growing, as Mrs. Ellington would have said, like weeds. Each time Maria saw them, they were changed; Kelly particularly. She was a pretty girl, willowy, with long, fine blond hair and china-blue eyes, with an upturned button nose and a haughty curl to her lip. Maria was proud of her as of a beautiful vase, but Kelly, whose character seemed drawn more from her mother than from her father, and who favored skimpy skirts and revealing singlets that recalled her mother in youth, was not loving to Maria, did not encourage a connection. It was Paul, still Radek's child, who chattered cheerfully to his grandmother on the telephone, who embraced and caressed her when they met. As for Anita, Maria could not help but speak of her to Mrs. Ellington (to whom else could she have spoken?), even though she kept always in the back of her mind her employer's plaint about her "incessant talking."

At about the same time as Mrs. Ellington's eruption, Anita had renounced her job at the tachometer plant. Without explanation she had, according to Radek, progressively renounced everything: housekeeping, shopping, cooking, and eventually dressing as well. She grew, so Radek said, enormous, and neglected to dye, or even to wash, her hair, so that it stuck, in greyed clumps, to her head. According to Radek, Anita lounged on the sofa in her purple furry robe with the remote control beneath one hand and an array of drinks and sweet foods beneath the other. She moved only as far as the kitchen to replenish her stores, her once scrawny frame lumbering and anguished. At night, she stayed planted there while the others made life, and supper, around her; and she fell asleep there, too, with the television flickering, washing her pale bulk in its violet rays. This, at least, was the picture Rod painted for Maria, or the picture that she designed for herself from his despairing, near-Delphic pronouncements.

Not that Maria ever saw for herself any of this disintegration: there were no invitations at all to Oakville, let alone to the cottage on Lake of Bays, and when the family came to Markham Street, they came without Anita, and made only the flimsiest pretexts for her absence.

"Mom doesn't feel too good," Paul would whisper, and Maria, looking around at the three of them, would see all eyes averted—Kelly pondering her own image on the wall, Paul fiddling with the plastic covering on the chesterfield, Radek feigning interest in the street outside—and all expressions blank.

Maria suffered for her son and grandchildren, but felt no sympathy at all for her daughter-in-law. "Her mother was a pig, now she's turning into a pig," she said to Mrs. Ellington.

"It sounds like she's seriously depressed, Maria. Is she seeing a doctor? It sounds like she should see a doctor."

"She's not sick, she's lazy."

"She may be that too, but it sounds to me as though she must be depressed."

"What's she got to be depressed about? Beautiful house, and kids, and no need to be working? I worked every day of my life, Mrs. Ellington, and I'm not depressed."

"Maybe that's *why* you're not depressed!"

Maria shook her head. "She's not a nice girl, Anita. She was never a nice girl. I'm sorry for my Radek, that she's like this, but it's no surprise. She's no good."

"Still, you might suggest she see a doctor, when you speak to Radek. Just suggest it."

Maria would do no such thing. She had never intervened, not back when she should have, when first the scraggly trollop had appeared in her kitchen, nor later when the engagement had been announced. She didn't hold much faith in doctors: she had faith in the power of movement, in the necessity of continuing. And there was no way to impart faith of that kind to a creature who had never had it.

By the time of Mrs. Ellington's blood-streaked walls, in August of 1993, matters in Oakville had gone from bad to worse. Maria told herself that it was all because Anita's mother had never taught her how to keep house, as if all order would stem from the material, working its way back into the spirits of the inhabitants: when Maria recalled her childhood village, and her parents' cottage in Gulyaypole, she recalled poverty, to be sure, and clutter, and the random, rank odors of a life without sewerage, but in her memory it was a world of cleanliness, of boiled sheets and scrubbed fingers, and the landscape a vast snow-blanketed plain on which the black dog of her imagining was the only sullying blot. Problems like those that beset Radek and his family made no sense to her, they had no logic. They could never, in her cosmos, have transpired.

Mrs. Ellington's difficulties, however, she apprehended immediately, and she knew that it was not a matter of lack of will, it was, willy-nilly, a force greater than Mrs. Ellington, greater than Maria: it was a force of ending. Mrs. Ellington's change of temper, two years before, appeared premonitory in this light, a warning.

And although Maria asked her employer to tell Judith to call her, Mrs. Ellington had still sufficient will to be stubborn. She did not. Judith did not call. Having no one with whom to share her anxieties (what interest could Radek possibly have in the old woman's plight, when his own family languished in such disarray, without even supper on the table unless he stopped at the Pizza Hut or Kentucky Fried Chicken on the way home?), Maria harbored them close, sat with them in her pristine, familiar living room at night. They troubled her sleep: again and again, in those brief weeks, she dreamed of the bloodstained walls, and saw in her imagination Mrs. Ellington's mangled corpse, so that when she awoke she had to restrain herself from ringing the Manley Avenue apartment (at 4 a.m., at dawn) to reassure herself that the old woman breathed still. In her dreams, as she told Lev on the sultry Sunday afternoon when she knelt to arrange a jar of yellow daisies at his head, the strange thing about the apartment was that it was empty: no furniture, no pictures, not even any carpet on the concrete floors. Everything was white, sterile as the hospital in which Lev, so many years before, had expired. And yet, she knew it was Mrs. Ellington's flat, and she knew, with a rabid and dreadful certainty, that the blood on the walls was Mrs. Ellington's, that the corpse which would await her—each night, she recognized the scene, but could not prevent it from unfolding—was Mrs. Ellington's as well, satin bed jacket and all.

When Judith did finally appear—a swift, four-day jaunt to see the dentist: in spite of all her years in California, she still had her teeth tended in Toronto—Maria fell upon her as though Mrs. Ellington were already genuinely dead.

"You can't see it now," she said of the blood, "because I scrubbed with Javelle water. But Judith, every night I see it. It was terrible. You can't let her die like that."

Judith sighed, long, buckling gulps of air. "She's ninety-two, you know, Maria. We're all getting old, I guess. I've known, for a while—sometimes, on the phone, she says things and I think . . . but I suppose I've tried to ignore them. I wanted to pretend. But I've got to do something about it."

Judith extended her stay. She told Maria that when she had said to her mother that she would have to leave the flat, Mrs. Ellington—a woman formerly so full of fight—had not even protested. Maria's eyes teared at this news, at the memory of Mrs. Ellington's bitter railing two years before, which now seemed a frail image, a last gush of bile from an emptied source. Judith went alone to investigate homes for the aged: from a list of eleven, she narrowed the possibilities to three, and these three she invited Maria to come to see with her. Maria agreed.

"I know what she likes," she observed, although she knew

that this was not entirely true: their way of knowing each other was at once excruciatingly intimate and oddly formal; and while Mrs. Ellington might have said that she knew Maria's tastes, after almost fifty years, Maria would have known that for a partial truth. Similarly, she knew there were sides of Mrs. Ellington, surfaces, which remained perforce undisclosed to her, in spite of all the years. And yet "I know what she likes" was heartfelt: what detail of Mrs. Ellington's daily living needs did Maria not hold? That she slept propped on three pillows; that she drank her breakfast juice before her toast and coffee; that she preferred minted dental tape to plain dental floss—Maria knew it all.

This knowledge, far more pervasive than Judith's, proved only marginally relevant in the visitation of the old folks' homes. It was a question of choosing between grimnesses: "I don't know, Judith," Maria said after each foray into the age- and disinfectant-scented corridors, through which billowed occasional gusts of institutional cooking odors and urine. "Seems like it would make Mrs. Ellington depress, living here."

Until finally Judith, in her exasperation, clucked, "Of course it is; of course it will. But what choice have we got? You said yourself, it's palpably clear, she simply can't manage. So we choose one. Please, Maria," she implored. "Help me choose one."

"It's like the camps, in the war," observed Maria. "Mrs. Ellington doesn't get to choose. Only for Mrs. Ellington, it's clear: she's going to die there. I never thought I was going to die, but many people did, old people, sick people. But I could manage because I knew, no way, I was not going to die there.

Later, you know, in the factory, I thought maybe I would die, with the bombs. I was so scared. So I run away. But in the camp, I knew. But Mrs. Ellington, she knows she's going in this place to die. She knows it like I knew I wouldn't let it." Maria paused. She looked Judith in the eye, outside the double doors of the third old people's home. A scrawny ancient with a vacant smile perched behind Judith on a bench, in his singlet, as bony and haggard as the workers in the camps. "I can't help you choose, Judith. I can't do that to Mrs. Ellington. I'm sorry."

Judith chose Humber Lodge. It was small, relatively new, and not far from Manley Avenue.

"She'll still be in the neighborhood," Judith reasoned. "She's lived in this part of the city all her life."

Judith also liked the West Indian woman who was the matron at Humber Lodge. "She's very outgoing, Maria, so friendly. Approachable, you know? She really seems to care."

"I don't know, Judith," said Maria. "Mrs. Ellington doesn't like friendly, so much. She's not always wanting to talk to people. They bug her, you know. And Judith"—Maria was awkward, but said it anyway—"Mrs. Ellington doesn't so much like black people, you know."

Judith gaped. "Nonsense. My mother's not racist."

"It's not that, it's . . ." But it was. Maria knew it for a fact, but she could tell Judith didn't want to know. "Never mind," she said. "I'm sure Humber Lodge is fine. It's close by Lev," she added. "So I can come easily. I know the way."

The rooms at Humber Lodge were essentially furnished, and Judith moved Mrs. Ellington in on October 1. She didn't need much: her clothes, her books on tape, her transistor radio.

She didn't take any photographs, because she couldn't see them anyway, but she took her familiar scented soap, and her mohair rug, and her satin bed jacket. She asked Judith to provide a little fridge, in which she might keep snacks of her own, and juice; but she did not take the teapot, and Maria realized that Mrs. Ellington would never again propose to her, in that particular tone of voice she knew so well, "Cup of tea, Maria?"

Indeed, as it fell to Maria to disassemble Mrs. Ellington's apartment alongside Judith—it had to be sold to pay the cost of the nursing home—she felt the weight of ending painfully across her ribs. It seemed, for the first time, as she piled books into boxes and wrapped plates with newspaper, as she removed paintings from walls and filled a vast trunk with Mrs. Ellington's linen (including the poor, bleach-spattered towels her employer had ruined during Maria's absence), that she could not draw breath fully into her lungs. She felt old, and sore, and weak. Judith was not throwing anything away—"I couldn't possibly, Maria. Not as long as my mother is *living*"—but rather was putting it all in storage: the high, stiff marriage bed, the scratched but glossy breakfast table, the Noah's Ark platter, and even the doilies, Mrs. Ellington's precious round doilies, tatted by some Scottish ancestor in some other distant place. It wasn't enough, though, to know that Mrs. Ellington's belongings still existed. It had been their disposition, their almost-religious order, whose perfection it had been Maria's life's work to maintain, that represented, more than represented, somehow *contained*, Mrs. Ellington. In emptying the apartment, it was as if they took the vessel bearing Mrs. Ellington's lifeblood and turned it upside down over a patch of earth.

When they were done, the two women who had known one another for so much of their lives, who were not, after all, so far apart in age, both of them senior citizens themselves, stood, in the wan but clear October light, surveying the apartment in its naked whiteness.

"It's like my dream, Judith. It's terrible to see."

"It doesn't seem like much, after all, a life," agreed Judith, with her arms wrapped tight around herself. "But the lucky thing is, we've still got Mother. We haven't lost Mother."

Maria, not so sure, did not reply.

Judith stayed a little while longer, with friends on the far side of town—up near Mount Pleasant cemetery, where Mrs. Ellington would eventually join her husband—and as long as she did stay, she picked Maria up at Markham Street on Tuesday mornings (although not until nine-thirty or so) and took her out to Humber Lodge to visit Mrs. Ellington.

Maria detested these visits. She would have preferred a month on Radek's motorboat in the middle of Lake of Bays. She would have preferred almost anything. From the moment the double doors opened, there was the assault upon the senses, the cloying smells and undertones of the institution. There was the garrulous director, the woman Judith had so admired, with her false bonhomie and surreptitious impatience. There was a resident dog—a vast, rumbling black Labrador tricked out with a red neckerchief, who reminded Maria alternately of Jack McDonald's obstreperous, caress-hungry Sport, and of the goitered black canine of her memories of Gulyaypole—whose supposed purpose was to disseminate good cheer among the inmates but who, to Maria, seemed only an insistent announcement of their

mortality: how could the aged look at this creature, barely beyond puppyhood, and not feel it was gloating openly, ambling
among them all in its garish scarf and saying, "Look at me, a
mere dog: I will outlive you."

She did not mention this dog to Mrs. Ellington, who, after
all, was too blind to see him. She did not know, on those visits,
what to talk about, and Mrs. Ellington, too, never before at a
loss for words, verged on muteness. She did not, as Maria had
known she would not, take to Humber Lodge: after a tablemate
expired of a heart attack over his watery minestrone, she refused to leave her room for meals, and insisted that they be
brought up to her on a tray. She appeared to Maria shrunken
and husklike, her tiny frame closed in upon itself, her movements faltering. She let herself go, failed to wash or brush her
hair; failed, some mornings, to dress at all. Her only insistent
flame of selfhood was the tenacity with which she played her
transistor radio, apparently in spite of her neighbors' com-
plaints. It was invariably on when Judith and Maria arrived,
and Mrs. Ellington left it chattering while her daughter tidied
busily around her, arranging flowers or washing out the bathroom sink, or tugging with Mrs. Ellington's old blue plastic
hairbrush at her sparse and matted curls. If their visit coincided
with the news, she would shush them—although often they
sat in silence anyway—and would nod thoughtfully, her unseeing eyes focused somewhere in the middle distance, while the
world's, or the city's, tragedies were imparted.

They did not then discuss the news, as they might have
done on Manley Avenue; they did not discuss Radek and Anita
either, nor young Kelly and Paul; and when, only once, Mrs.

Ellington bothered to ask after them, Maria lied and said they were fine, because she had, in her mind, started to describe Anita's reportedly grim state and been painfully struck by how clearly it seemed to mirror Mrs. Ellington's. It seemed, in Humber Lodge as in Oakville, that the one thing that must absolutely not be acknowledged was the most glaring thing of all: ending. At any price—Maria had rarely lied, in her life, and did not like to do so—it must not be openly accorded the place that it had usurped nonetheless.

All around Maria, there was ending. Not, as with the war so long before, in the manner of a promise; but mere ending. Disorder. Judith departed, to rejoin her husband, her life in California. The Grand Palais, at the end of that November, shut its peeling doors for the last time, to make way for an exclusive Lakeshore club, of the sort that, many years before, Leah Makerevich or Judith Ellington herself might have frequented, for swimming and for tennis. Maria was not as regretful as she might have expected: since the dull ache in her ribs, the sorrow, had begun, she no longer felt the urge to push out alone into the cold Saturday-night air, and no longer desired to spin and be spun across the ice-smooth parquet. The red and blue lights of the dance hall had come to seem tawdry, even malevolent: she had only recently noticed that they made everyone in the room look sick.

Ending was coming to Oakville, too. A week before Christmas, Kelly, fifteen, ran away from home with her twenty-two-year-old boyfriend, a lover her parents had not known to exist. The couple was traced to a seedy motel in Muskoka, because

Kelly was charging their room to her father's credit card; and although Radek drove up—alone—to retrieve her, she refused to come until the police were called, and assured her, hands at their belts, that she must.

Maria, upon hearing this news, remembered Tagomack in winter, the mountainous egg white of the drifts, and the cold air like a metal tube all the way down to her heart. She remembered the black menace of the pines there at dusk. And she remembered the opposite of ending, Lev's thawing cheek against her own upon his return to the cabin, and the round, soft flesh of tiny Radek's arms gleaming by the fire after his nightly bath. It was when she remembered these things, which had been hope, that she started to cry. Radek, at the end of the telephone line, telling her about Kelly, thought it was his daughter's disobedience and the shame of her fugue that brought on the tears, and Maria did not have the heart to disabuse him; that she expected no better of Kelly—wholly Anita's child— seemed better left unsaid.

At Christmas, there was no invitation to Oakville: how could there have been? Radek and Paul ventured, solemn and manly, to Markham Street, bearing a poinsettia and a bottle of perfume. They sat, man and boy, on either side of Maria over the Santa Claus cloth, and picked at the turkey she had prepared—it was, in truth, a bit dry: she still, after so long, did not have the Canadian habit of Christmas, and would have cooked vareniki and blintzes, in her own tradition, were it not that the boy was squeamish and would not have eaten. They stayed until after dark, and for once Maria did not tremble with the sense that her children wanted to leave her. But she knew this had less to do with her company (they didn't talk much; they put on the television and sat before it, three abreast, crinkling the sofa's plastic coating) than with their reluctance to go home. She thought she knew, now, how they felt—how they had always felt—about visiting her; she imagined that they felt as she did at Humber Lodge: silenced, uneasy, unable to bring their lives into the room with them, for fear of disrupting its order, an order of lies, of what could not be acknowledged.

Of what, for Maria, did these lies consist? She looked around her living room and tried to see it as Radek and Paul must. A mausoleum, a hollow protectorate. Nothing had altered since Radek had left home, so many years before, except the creeping amoeba of family photographs along the wall. Everything else—Lev's chair!—stayed rooted exactly in its place, pickled and protected in its swaddling of plastic. It was not an atmosphere of ending; it was as if everything had ended, long before. In seeking to preserve her life, in all its precious meaning, she had prevented life from entering. She had scrubbed and tidied around it, had skirted the present in the hope that it would remain full of the past. She had not thought of herself as nostalgic; she had not thought of herself as pointlessly lonely; but when, in a sudden flood, her son and grandson on either side of her, she felt herself slipping under their skins and into their thoughts, she suddenly saw herself as a prisoner, an unknowable husk. The weight upon her ribs—it seemed that she could feel each one, each knobbled rise beneath her blouse—was almost intolerable. But there was nothing to be said, and she allowed the television to speak for her, and when Radek and Paul rose to leave she pressed the turkey carcass upon them, neatly bound in foil, and kissed them lightly on each cheek, as she would always have done.

In January, Radek told her that he and Anita had decided to divorce. Kelly, who had not spoken to her father directly since that evening in Muskoka and who had—he was quite sure of it—been climbing out of her bedroom window at night to tryst with her unsuitable lover, would remain with her mother. Anita and Kelly were both quite decided on this plan, Radek said, and there seemed little purpose in fighting them.

"Just like Anita with her mother, nah?" said Maria. "No, Radek, I have to tell you something, and you'll forgive me, I'm hoping. I should have said it a long time ago. She's not a nice girl, that Anita."

"She's unhappy, Mom. I guess I couldn't make her happy, in the end."

"She's not worth it, Radek. She's no good."

"You don't know her, Mom. You never liked her. It's too late now. But we'll find a way to go on. Somehow, we'll find a way."

"Who's living in the house, then?"

"I want Anita to have it. She chose all the furniture. It's her house, really. It doesn't matter to me."

"And the cottage? And the boat?"

"We're selling. I'll put it on the market in the spring."

Maria made a chucking sound. "You hardly went there. Maybe three, four times?"

"It seemed like the cottage was the beginning of the end, Mom. I don't know why. It was supposed to be the beginning."

He gave a bitter little laugh. "Anyway, Mom, it doesn't matter. Don't be upset. Everything'll work out somehow."

"You can come here, you know."

"Huh?"

"You and Paul. Come live here. It makes good sense, nah?"

"I don't know, Mom. We'll see what happens. It's nice of you to offer, but—I don't know right now."

"Well, that's okay. I don't know either. Maybe I'm not going to Cuba this year, so . . . everything's up in the air."

"Not going to Cuba? But you always go, Mom."

"Maybe it's time for something different. We'll see."

In the event, Maria did not go to Cuba. She missed it—she knew the exact week in March and, when it came, felt the cold Toronto air particularly through each of the seven days, thinking of the dawn over the sand, and her private seabirds (although she hadn't seen the birds for years; somehow, sometime, they, too, had moved on to other bays)—but she did not regret her choice. She spent the week removing the now clouded plastic from the furniture in her living room, and rolling the vinyl matting up off the floor. On the Sunday which would, in other years, have been the day of her return from Cuba, she went, on a whim, to an art sale at the Howard Johnson's near the waterfront, which she had seen advertised on television, and carried home with her on the streetcar a painting that she bought there, wrapped in brown paper. The package was cumbersome, and she was sweating with the effort by the time she reached the house; but flushed with excitement, she tore the paper from the picture before even removing her coat, and left the wrapping crumpled on the sofa while she admired her purchase.

It was a large painting, easily three feet long, of a tropical sunset. The colors were brighter than any others in the Markham Street house—they were almost Cuban colors: pink and orange and a light, greeny-blue—but she thrilled to their riotousness the way she thrilled to Cuban music, and she hung the painting on the dining room wall, where the late-afternoon light would fall upon it all year round and illuminate the white gulls soaring, like sweeping parentheses, across the glowing horizon. She had never done such a thing before.

When she next went to visit Mrs. Ellington, she felt that she at last had something to tell her. The old woman was bent over in her chair. She mostly kept her eyes shut, by then, because she said it made no difference—"I can't tell day from night, Maria. Day from night"—and her feet were propped, like items separate from her body, upon a little stool. Her ankles were grotesquely swollen, ballooned at the end of her little withered legs, and she wore over her once dainty insteps sheepskin slippers that would not rub against the suppurating sores which had burst, in antique rebellion, onto her tight and shiny heels. Her breathing was raspy and shallow, which Maria could hear because Mrs. Ellington did not, for once, have her radio turned on. "Same old, same old," Mrs. Ellington muttered when Maria asked about the silence. "And I said to myself, frankly, what's the point?"

"I bought a painting, Mrs. Ellington."

"Why'd you do that?"

"Because I saw it and I liked it. It makes me happy, the colors, nah?"

Mrs. Ellington nodded. She scrunched her eyes more tightly shut. After a moment, she said, "Describe it for me, Maria? Is it pretty?"

So Maria described it. She described the pale gold swath of sand in the foreground, the way the paint was lumpy and textured there to give the genuine impression of the ridges, the way they stood out to the eye but melted beneath your toes when you walked barefoot. She described the burning smells that drifted out from inland, and the salty air that floated in off the sea. She described the calls of the hawkers and the roosters' intermittent crowing. She described the way the water foamed, in tiny, excited bubbles, as it slid up over the smoothed, dark sand, and the way it ran around the shells and pebbles as if drawing muscled musical notes, on its way back out. She described the heat of the beach, the miasma that lingered even till sunset, when it seemed tangibly to float, in alternating layers, with the cool, just as in the water there were pockets of cold among the warm, little hidden, invigorant explosions. She described the breadth of the bay, the darkening blue of the sea as it deepened away from land in a subaqueous valley, the smoothness of the sea strokes in the painting and the way they conveyed the porcelain flatness of the indigo stretch in a windless dusk. She described the glow of the sun, like a fiery bulb on the horizon, and its mantle of roseate hues, reaching out in overlapping swirls and tendrils, as far as the eye could see. And lastly, she described the gulls soaring there, wavering slightly on the high current, appearing and disappearing, white, fine, gone, depending on the light and on their arcing in the sky.

When she was done, Maria folded her hands in her lap and looked at Mrs. Ellington, tiny in her armchair. The old woman had fallen asleep while Maria was speaking, and her breaths were deeper, more steady; but Maria imagined, as she tiptoed away, that she glimpsed a smile on Mrs. Ellington's lips, and in the loosening of her features, an opening to relief.

The Hunters

Hypocrite lecteur, mon semblable, mon frère.

—BAUDELAIRE

At one time not so very long ago, for reasons that would not be worth explaining, I found myself temporarily installed in a flat on the outer reaches of London's Maida Vale. The area would more honestly have been called Kilburn, but the estate agent doubtless feared that the exorbitant rent, calculated precisely to attract foreigners such as myself to her properties (on the misguided but dearly held principle that you get what you pay for), was frankly irreconcilable with the word "Kilburn," which evoked to the even superficially informed visitor teetering tooth-less Irishmen and snarling pit bull terriers looming against a backdrop of garish discount shops, fly-kissed butchers' displays and cratered pavement.

This stereotypical view was not, entirely, unfounded, and had the estate agent so much as whispered the word "Kilburn" to me, I would doubtless have found the fluttering polyester scarves and soaped windows of the nearby High Road less quaint and more menacing than, in the event, I did. But when she showed me the flat—she was a shy girl of twenty-two or -three, with a perfectly groomed plait and a rash of red spots about her chin, which vulnerability somehow, seemingly (and falsely, as of course it transpired) rendered her incapable of dissimulation—I believed her when she said it was in Maida Vale and, having no idea where Kilburn was in relation to that Elysian field, or vale, indeed, and, it has to be said, misled by the sunlight glittering through the trees and by the newly painted portico, I failed even to bat an eye when we passed in front of the rather sordid establishment draped in green velvet called The New Kilburn Tandoori.

I admit it: I was foolish. I was taken in by the high rent. I had been looking for some days and was losing patience with my drab, ill-smelling and overpriced Paddington hotel. Besides which, the real estate agent told me—and this was her only out-and-out lie, but a significant one, which I hold against her and on account of which I wish upon her an eternal rash of spots—that the canal of Little Venice, that delicious and serene attraction which is sufficiently untouristed for each tourist to consider that he has discovered it for himself, and which was my primary reason for seeking a flat in Maida Vale rather than in Hampstead or Chelsea or in centrally located but oft-overlooked and quietly mournful Pimlico—she told me that the canal was but a few short blocks away. She may not have said "short." She certainly said "a few blocks." And it was only after signing the lease that I would discover I had to walk a good twenty arm-swinging minutes on the steamy pavement (it was summer, with my toes and fingers swelling and the diesel-drenched air blackening my mucus membranes), along the klaxon-riddled, drill-thrummed upper reaches of the Edgware Road (from just above, as we are frank, the moment where it becomes the Kilburn High Road) to reach the canal. And when I did, perhaps because I was cross and hot, perhaps because it was summer, the canal appeared less delicious and serene than I had remembered it, and could more accurately have been described (to my jaded eye) as dank and murky, a black and brackish stretch of water upon which drifted leaves and plastic detritus, rather closer to a sewage tank than to the Venetian idyll of my recall. After that one grim visit, I avoided Little Venice for the rest of my months in London, even after the weather became London-like again, damp and brisk and grey. I did not go back there—although I went past, obviously, on the bus and in taxis upon occasion—and although I am a changed person I have not been back there to this day.

But really, I took the flat because it pleased me. That would be the honest answer, if I catapult myself back to the late-May afternoon of my visit with the estate agent—Sheila, her name was: Sheila Cooke. Whatever happened after that changed my feelings about the place—and a great deal happened, although in a way nothing did—I cannot pretend that I was diddled into taking it under false pretenses. It somehow spoke to me. There is no need to go into the why of it, but I was sad at that time, and very much on my own, and the apartment had the feeling of a place where people had been happy. Most of the other furnished lets I had seen had no aura whatsoever, just the relentless hideousness of their furnishings and the spartan utilitarianness of their kitchen cupboards, with a little stack of ill-assorted plates and a clutch of tin forks. But this flat, which consisted of a small entrance, a large living room, a bedroom, and a separate, sizeable kitchen in which one could sit, felt like a home. Or like part of a home—which, strictly speaking, it had been. It was on the first floor (in the British sense) at the back of a large house now divided up into flats. It had high ceilings, and wooden floors, across which were laid colorful kilims, and all the rooms were dominated by immense, very clean windows, plate glass expanses stretching from hip height upwards, like an artist's studio, filling the flat with light, and a feeling of air, of openness, which in that time I craved. The windows looked over the garden that belonged to the residents downstairs—a riot of peonies and lilies and climbing clematis, shaded by an ancient apple tree—and over all the other gardens, in both directions, left and right, and again over the fence at its foot. It looked at all the other houses, too, beyond the gardens, the houses opposite, which were, from its vantage, like dolls' houses, through the windows of which people like dolls could be seen to lead their doll-like lives.

All the furniture in the apartment, although there wasn't much of it, was tasteful, as though it had been chosen by a person who would have wanted to live there; and all the appliances in the kitchen were new. The bathroom had a white tub, and navy tiles, and a flattering light; and in summertime it didn't matter that its narrow window would not completely shut. But it was the kitchen table, a broad, solid, scratched old thing with paint flaking off its rounded legs, with the suggestion of society around it, that decided me. I was at a time in which I desired exactly that: the suggestion of society, without its actual impingement into my carefully controlled existence. This is why, also, the people flitting among their trappings in the houses opposite so appealed to me: they were at once there and not there, a sign that life continued, even if it had nothing to do with me.

I took the place for just over three months, which was possible because the rates were set by the week. I signed and produced a bankers' check that very sunlit afternoon, manifesting a zeal which seemed rather to disconcert young Sheila Cooke. She had shown me quite a few places before that one, almost a dozen in fact, and I had been politely noncommittal about all of them, which had led her to believe, I suspect, that I could not feel strongly about places, and that I would eventually and halfheartedly settle for the umpteenth apartment which would differ in no measurable regard from the first. She might have been right: I did not feel much up to caring, or had not thought that I did, until the moment, that afternoon, when I did suddenly care a good deal, which I took as a good sign at the time.

I was in London for the summer. I was there to research a book, my own. I was, needless to say, on my own, which had not been foreseen. Or should I say, it had been so only in a shadowy manner, for months prior to my departure: I was, officially, to have had a companion, and that remained the official state of affairs until a mere ten days before I flew across the Atlantic. There was no discernible progression, not discernible to the naked eye, from the state—coupled, as it were—in which the initial plan was made, to the state—uncoupled—in which ultimately I found myself: there was no marked deterioration of relations, there were no recordable rows, there was not even any unraveling of which one might have taken surreptitious note. No, the rupture came precisely as a rupture, an unforeseeable and inexplicable change, out, as we might have it, of the blue. Out of the blue, my plans changed. And yet, although this is the official version and, in every factual way the true version, there is also a version which is my own, and truer, or at least more true to me, although it would in no way and to no one be verifiable. That is to say, that if you had asked me, as far back as the new year—in strictest, almost unvoiceable confidence, as if, indeed, you were my alter ego, inside my head—if you had asked me whether I was to be accompanied on this prolonged research junket to London (which was already, then, at the turn of the year, of the century, of the millennium, very much in the offing), I would have said, "I somehow think not." I would never have said this aloud and did not, and in the event I cannot recall anyone asking, so I was never called upon to lie outright, and seeing as I did not commit this gut feeling to record prior to the events, there is no one but myself to assure you that this was indeed my feeling, not retrospectively, in light of what happened, but from the start. You will have to trust me on this. Because I later—in this time of which I speak, in this very flat in what was indisputably Kilburn—came to be obsessed with the irresolvable question of whether my gut feeling, as I call it, had been some sort of premonition of a truly unforeseeable disaster, or whether it had, in some quiet, seeping way, been the very cause of that disaster. Had I inadvertently—or worse, in some more profound way wholly deliberately—caused myself to come uncoupled, although I would have maintained, I would maintain still, that this was the last thing that I wanted? From the very moment in which it occurred to my unspoken heart of hearts that I might, that I would, have to travel alone, did it become my inescapable fate so to do? Was I the unwitting author of my own destruction?

But this, although it has its reasons, is not my focus here. This is not my purpose in turning an eye to my first summer of the third millennium—Godless, pace Malraux, as it was for me; although arguably, pace Malraux, it wasn't for me, at all— because my purpose is not my own story. This was, as I hope I make clear, a time in which I had no life. Or rather, in which I had no life that could be seen. Indeed, some evenings in my Kilburn flat, with the lights off, watching the doll-like neighbors opposite gesticulating or moving from room to room, I felt more than invisible (which to them, most surely, I was); I felt God-like. Days, and more than once, entire weeks, would pass in which I had nothing more than perfunctory exchanges with minions of various descriptions—clerks and checkout girls and taxi drivers and librarians—and in which I knew that not one of them studied my face, nor even registered its features. Had I been called upon by the police to produce an alibi for one of these solitary days, I could not possibly have done so, because nobody saw me; even if they conversed with me, or pressed change or merchandise into my palms, I was and remain convinced that they did not see me.

Do not misunderstand me: I am not complaining of this. I did not feel sorry for myself, or certainly not on this account. If I say that I was sad, in that time, it is inescapably true, but it is also true that in my little round of days, hermetic and spare, from my flat to the British Library to my flat again, with forays to Marks and Spencer in the meantime (ah, the chicken korma platter! ah, the choux buns, two to a box!)—in those days I was positively exultant. I was sad, yes, I was on one level of my being, to be frank, almost suicidal (and unable to shake the preoccupation that I would die before my research was done, before my book was written), and at the same time, on another, I was blissful. I was happier than I had ever been, since early childhood. This made me think several things: one was that I had achieved a doglike state, that like an animal I was leading an unquestioning life, and that therein lay my pleasure. It was finite: I was in London only for the summer, after which I would return home. It was purposeful, or no more futile, at least, than any other time of my life, of any life. I was unencumbered. And this, this very unreflective euphoria which seemed to betoken an animal state, seemed also divine. I did feel God-like. I felt that I looked upon the mortals around me as from a great height. I observed anxiety or rage or hope in the faces of my fellows with a salutary flood of compassion; but it was as if their experience of life, so emotion-filled, so wearing, mired in the infinite, pointless encumberedness of their days, were completely other than mine. And my freedom from emotion, paradoxically, made me feel more rather than less alive; it made me feel, too, that they, all those who *felt*, were merely distracted by their feelings and were far less alive than I. I felt at once, and palindromically, like a dog and a god, and these were not contradictory experiences.

I also felt that I owed a great deal to the cocooning comforts of the flat that Sheila Cooke had found for me. Not

merely the southern exposure, which insistent light awakened
me on sunny mornings and, even on the greyest days, brought
an opalescent luminosity to the small, white bedroom; not
merely the aesthetic disposition of the furnishings and rugs; nor
still the ever-changing but ever-verdant pleasures of the flower
garden down below, from which stray and bonny bumblebees
wafted occasionally, noisily, upwards, on sweet-scented currents
of garden air—no, the greatest pleasures of the flat fell into
that category of the ineffable to which I have already made
reference: it felt as though people had been happy there. As
though, like sweat, or perfume, that happiness had suffused the
upholstery and misted upon the surfaces; or, like lint, as though
it lurked unreachable in the undusted corners.

Would I have been dismayed to learn that in fact a great
violence had been perpetrated in its rooms? Or that some miserable imprisonment had been suffered behind those pellucid
panes of glass? I think that in my initial God-like, doglike state,
I would simply not have believed it. The place, as it was first
known to me, which was the only way that I might know it,
was a place exuding happiness, no matter what complex of
emotions I brought, or signally failed to bring, within its four
walls. But all that could change. And would.

Ridley Wandor rang my doorbell at 8:20 p.m. on the first Friday
in July. It was the first time in my tenure that the doorbell had
been rung—or rather, that it had been rung by anyone other
than myself, who had rung it experimentally not long after I
moved in, in preparation for exactly such an eventuality, and in
order that I might recognize the ringing for the doorbell rather

than, say, a fire alarm or a hidden clock. It was a brutal and in-
vasive ringing, an assault rather than a serenade. I was, when
Ridley rang, nestled in at my favored kitchen table before a
plate of cold meats, cheese and salad and a bottle of crisp Vouvray, and with, as is my wont, my white linen napkin carefully
tucked into my collar, falling in a diamond formation over my
shirt. I had been relishing the twittering silence and the evening light in the trees, and the sips of my wine, and was, in truth,
reduced to trembling by the racket as I proceeded—stealthily,
on tiptoe—to the door. My hallway inside the flat was dark; I
thought, thereby, to remain unobserved while eyeing the person on the landing; but Ridley Wandor, perhaps thinking along
lines not unlike my own, had not pushed the timed light button in the hallway and must have negotiated the stairwell,
unwindowed as it was, in the greatest gloom. I could not see
a thing; or rather, could outline, in the penumbra, only an apparently significant, ungendered bulk, lurking motionless. Its
hand, as I peered, reached pudgily forward and pushed the bell
again, which activated the brutal clanging just above my head
and, in turn, regenerated my agitated trembling. Called back to
confront any world of direct human connection, however su-
perficial, I was neither God- nor doglike, but afraid.

In counteraction of which, I whipped my napkin from my
neck and dabbed my doubtless greasy lips; I flipped my inner
hall light switch and cleared my throat most authoritatively,
and asked, with as British an inflection as I could muster, "Who
is it?"

The voice—the minute, almost whispering voice, but flat,

disturbingly and unnaturally uninflected itself—proved unhelpful: "Ridley Wandor. It's Ridley Wandor."

I waited. I wondered how further to probe this apparition: "What do you want?" would have seemed to set a hostile tone; whereas "And who is Ridley Wandor?" showed more levity, and hence more intimacy, than I would have wished.

The creature spared me, in the event: "It's Ridley Wandor, your downstairs neighbor."

Whereupon I had little choice but to slip the bolt and open the door, loath though I was to do so. Perhaps because my intensive solitude had so neutralized my own emotional range, I found, in those weeks, that the emotional states of others emanated from them in waves, as powerfully as any scent. I could sense this on the buses, when breathless women flopped in beside me, in eagerness or fear; when men jittered their limbs in the bank queues, I could derive the manifold sources of their malaise; even teenagers, with their flouncing mannerisms and cardboard confidence, were laid bare to me at a glance, or a sniff. And Ridley Wandor, no teenager, was no exception, gave off the pewter tang of misery and the musk of menace. Oh, not to forget: and need. Acidic, brown. I can detect it even now as a recollected burning in my sinuses: the particular flavor of Ridley Iris Wandor.

She came in, in spite of the aura. She came in as far as the kitchen, where my delicious and private supper lay as bare and intimate to her roving eye as any nakedness. I did not want her in my kitchen. I did not want her to see my supper, suddenly sorrowful rather than jaunty, partially eaten on its plate, nor my wineglass, the sweat of which was broken by my fingerprints and mine alone. Let me be quite clear about this: from the instant that she appeared on the far side of my Judas hole, I was forced out of exultation and back into humanity, and I would have hated her for it no matter who she had been. But that she was both who she appeared and who she later proved to be—this proved inexcusable, wholly and utterly inexcusable to me. Far more so than, say, Sheila Cooke's quaint and false confusion between Maida Vale and Kilburn, or her out-and-out lie about the proximity of Little Venice: those were, to me, ultimately forgivable offenses. The existence, in my world—above all in my so pristinely sparse and meticulously evacuated London world, but in truth, in my world wheresoever it, and I, might be—and presence, more egregious still, of Ridley Wandor, was irredeemable, heinous, utterly unpardonable. I hated her the moment I set eyes on her, and all I ever wished was that she *would not be*.

For a start, she was ugly: pouchy, pallid, pig-eyed and all but lipless, indistinctly hulking in her lurid, swishing leisure gear, her colorless hair limp at the edges of her colorless face. Her age was, and remained, a mystery: she might have been in her late thirties, or in her early or even mid-fifties. Her skin had a slightly oily, preserved sheen that led me to assume she was older rather than younger, but I did not find out exactly until afterwards. Her hands looked as though they had been pillowed with water, white, veinless, unused hands, the nails of which were incongruously and alarmingly manicured, and painted—I recall the color so distinctly, a pearly shell-pink which on other fingers might have been alluring in its suggestive discretion but which, on Ridley Wandor, was offensive and grotesque. I noticed her hands because I could not bear to look too closely at her face, the ugliness of which resided not in any tangible, and hence admirable, disgrace, but in the lack it represented—lack of color, lack of distinction, lack of features. No eyebrows to speak of; no nameable hue to the blinking little eyes; no form to the little nose; as I have said, virtually no lips, and what slivers there were, bloodless. She did possess a jutting chin, a pale and, I would have said, Victorian chin, almost upwardly hooked like a Punch and Judy puppet's; but the ensemble made not for the sort of thrilling ugliness that so closely resembles, and sometimes outstrips, beauty: quite the opposite. She did not call out to be looked at but rather she *called out to be ignored*, and it was as if she knew it. I took her, almost mongoloid in appearance, to be stupid, but willful (the jutting chin being inseparable, in my vestigial and childish physiognomic assessments, from willfulness), and while the chin pointed me aright, I was, in underestimating her, a fool.

I noticed her hands, too, because in them she held a glass jar—of the sort bought in hardware stores for the putting up of preserves—in which were propped three stems of hollyhocks, thick, hairy and absurdly truncated, so that some of the garish pink flowers floundered, drowning in the water; but cut thus because otherwise the heavy stalks, too long, might have tipped the jar over. Intended, doubtless, to be fresh and pleasing, the hollyhocks in their receptacle were as mawkish and dumpy as the Frau—or rather, Fräulein—who brought them.

And still, when she tittered, the first release of that toneless and aggravating titter which I came to know so well, and said,

"These are for you," I did not sternly bid her remove them and herself, but rather smiled, the soul of politeness, and replied, "Why, thank you. Thank you very much."

"Mother and me, we thought you might like them. A bit of color, we said to ourselves, because you're on your own."

I noticed at once, and was displeased to, that they, the Wandors *mère et fille*, had observed my comings and goings sufficiently closely to know I was alone. "That was very thoughtful of you. I'd invite you to stay, but as you can see—"

She tittered again. "I wanted us to meet," she said. "I believe in being neighborly. I won't stay now—I've interrupted your supper. But perhaps you'll come down, soon, and meet mother, and the Hunters."

"The Hunters?" I could not imagine how two households might inhabit a flat the size of my own.

"That's what I call the rabbits. The Hunters. Although they're more like 'the hunted,' in this world, wouldn't you say?"

I smiled. I could sense that my smile was wan. It was as if her pallor were infecting me. I had, already, that brown, acidic taste in the back of my throat; the residue of my excellent Vouvray was lost. I did my best to usher her towards the door.

"Mother would have come with me," she said, shuffling and swishing reluctantly, having placed the jar of flowers on the kitchen table, perfectly centered, with a sinister care. "But she isn't very well. You know, age. The stairs are hard for her."

I nodded. "Please thank her nevertheless."

"I can't wait to tell her I've met you," she said, tittering again. "You're a professor, aren't you?"

I winced. "How did you know? Did Sheila Cooke say so?"

"I don't know Sheila. She's not upstairs, because upstairs is empty. No, we knew from the post, of course. On the table downstairs. The postman leaves the post on the table downstairs."

"Of course he does." I tried, again, to smile.

"Postwoman, actually. She. On our route, it's Esther, the regular. Lovely West Indian lady. She leaves it there."

"Certainly. And thank you. And good night."

Even when she had gone, it was as if she were still in the room. My supper was ruined—not that it had gone cold, because cold it had always been, but because it had no longer any taste for me. The evening had ceased to be rosy and was falling into darkness, and in order to see my food I was forced to light the kitchen—a sulfurous light, sterile and unlovely; which, moreover, transformed me, to some invisible voyeur, into precisely the staged and preposterous mobile figurine which so entertained me in the houses opposite. As for the hollyhocks: they gave off a faint odor of vegetable matter, swampy and unclean, and I was actively repelled by their hirsute trunks, as by the lone ant that journeyed down one stem and made his busy, hesitant and futile way around and around the jar's rim, until I took a God-like mercy and squashed him with my forefinger. This disgusting non-arrangement of non-flowers, this aesthetic blight upon my dinner table, how can I explain to you that it *was*, iconically, Ridley Wandor? It was as if she had left her photograph winking at me on the table; as if I knew—I did know, of course I knew; whether that knowing was a premonition or a predetermination—that I would not be able to escape her. That the assault of the doorbell, which had so set me to trembling, was but the first of many such assaults; that she, for all her cloddishness, for all I could not have described her in any way other than by what she *did not have*, for all I could not have put an age, nor barely, a gender upon her; for all she seemed more emphatically *not to be* than I did, I knew her for the stronger. Sly, insinuating, persistent, but passive, ever passive, she would—I knew it from the titter—sink her jaws into my little life and insist—upon it, upon herself, upon her presence in it—with all the vigor of a hyena at carrion. What I am saying is that I knew at once—and how I hated her for it— that she had ruined my London summer, that she had shattered my equanimity, and that she would not let go. I had become the hunted, and I made no mistake about it, even then.

It was some days before I had to see her again. The lull, and a burst of rain—days of soporific drizzle, on several of which I forewent my routine foray to the library and locked myself in the opalescent bedroom with a stack of books, pretending that it was wintertime and that I was ill; and who was there to contradict me? Not even the telephone rang—all helped me to imagine that Ridley Wandor had been but a figment, an unfortunate hallucination of my overly tired mind. I was living, with my books, in another century, in another realm, and it was entirely possible that I had merely dreamt—my dreams had always been unnaturally vivid—and then given full rein to my solipsism. In sum, I decided I would rather believe my sanity shaky than allow that my distress, after Ridley Wandor's visit, had been based upon anything real.

But when next I saw her—in broad daylight, on the Kilburn High Road, emerging from one of those murky junk shops whose merchandise is plastic tat of innumerable types and uncategorizable vileness, each item more useless than the last— there could be no doubt that she was no figment. People clearly saw her—although I imagined that they, like me, could not bring themselves to look at her—and she had, clanking at her side, plastic bags full of purchases that were undoubtedly real— as real as the Kilburn High Road itself.

"Hello, you!" she cried, as if we were the greatest of friends, and projected her titter so loudly that it emerged as a guffaw. "Fancy meeting you here!"

"Marks and Spencer," I muttered, between clenched teeth. "On my way home from work."

"I'm on my way home too."

"I'm on my way to Marks and Spencer."

"Shame. Shame. Mother's waiting. I'd better fly. She hasn't seen me, of course, in four whole days."

"Four days?"

"Four whole days. That's how I work, you see, four days on and three days off. Four on, three off."

I nodded, measuring the curtness of the gesture, limning rudeness. She didn't appear to notice. She put her shopping bags down on the pavement. A red plastic bowl emerged from the side of one, like a snail from its shell.

"Aren't you going to ask what I do?"

"But of course." I kept my eyes on the central navy stripe of her soiled pink and blue shell suit. It did not immediately occur to me that the amorphous expanse upon which I trained my gaze was, in fact, her bosom; and when it did, I felt my face color from the roots of my hair. "Please, tell me what you do?"

Ridley tittered. "Guess!"

"No, really. I can't."

"Just try."

"Please, Miss Wandor. I—" I looked around for an excuse, in the late-afternoon clutter of the High Road. A burst of diesel cloud enveloped us, from a passing 28. Beneath the diesel, my nostrils were rank with the smell of hot, raw meat from the neighboring butcher stall, where the steaks and chops were marinated, all day long, in bus fumes. "My shopping," I said. "Your mother."

"Mrs. W's waiting, it's true. So I'll give you a hint: it's the caring business."

"Caring? Business?"

"Oh, you are a silly," she tittered again, just as a determined old lady with a plaid trolley barged sharply into her elbow. But Ridley Wandor, unfazed, merely caressed her offended limb with abstracted tenderness, and continued to speak, oblivious to the passing octagenarian's hawkish scowl. "The caring business. I take care of people. Actually"—she leaned in, confidentially—"I take care of the aged."

"How admirable."

"I know what you're thinking—"

"Oh yes?"

"You're thinking, 'But she already takes care of Mrs. W, who is aged enough'—but she isn't really, you know. Barely twenty when she had me. Her health's not the best, but she isn't—"

"Miss Wandor, my shopping—"

"Of course. And my mum! It does her no good to have me up on the High Road just talking about her!"

"Quite."

She picked up her shopping bags and moved as if to cross the street.

"Good-bye then." I waved, brightly.

She turned back with sudden intensity. "It's not a home. You should know that. I don't believe in them—for Mother, for example? I never could. No, it's at their houses, to help them stay at home."

"I see." Although I didn't.

"One at a time. I go to them four days a week for as long as they need me."

"Of course."

"Then they die, you understand." She said this very fiercely.

"They're old," I conceded.

"And unwell. That's why they need me."

"Of course."

"Then they die in the end," she whispered, with a widening of her little eyes, and her eerie titter.

"As do we all, as do we all." She guffawed. "But not today, Miss Wandor. Let's hope not today."

On my own in my sunlit flat, I found myself listening. Against my will, listening. Not that very much noise seeped its way up to me. Occasionally, of an evening, when their garden doors were open, and my windows also, I would hear the twang of Wandor *fille* and a deep, intermittent thrum, always fainter, that I took to be the echo of her mother. Sometimes, sitting in the kitchen, I could see Ridley Wandor, in one of her three shell suits and always, always, wearing long sleeves, no matter the weather, pottering among the plants with a watering can or secaturs. Her movements were doughy and listless: she did not garden with the vim of one entranced by nature. And yet the plantings blossomed abundantly at her hands.

Once, I was interrupted in my reading by great hooplah, Ridley's voice raised and thundering steps outside, and I peered from my perch to see her galumphing in pursuit of not one, not two, but three flop-eared, wide-eyed plump but agile rabbits, one white and two of that dun color one associates with rabbit slippers. She proved herself more limber than one might have expected, and lunged far into the shrubbery to retrieve them, one by one; after which there wafted up the sounds of besotted scolding and—unless I imagined it—the clanging of their cages.

Through all this, Wandor *mère* never, as far as I could tell, stepped out even as far as the swept patio. And in the days when Ridley Wandor was out—"caring"—I heard nothing from the flat at all, not even the muted reverberations of the television set.

I began to wonder about Mrs. Wandor. I grew extremely curious. I had not seen her; I could not, with certainty, claim to have heard her. It would be more accurate, perhaps, to say that I began to wonder about Ridley Wandor herself: I wondered whether she had made her mother up. Mrs. Wandor might be living in Liverpool, for all I knew; she might not be living at all. If, as Ridley had said, the mother had given birth to Ridley at twenty, and Ridley, though her age was, as I have said, oddly indeterminate, could not reasonably be much older than forty-five, then the mother wasn't old at all, was barely a senior citizen. In which case, I found myself asking, what could be the nature of her infirmity? What kept her from stepping even so far as the patio of her back garden? Unless, I found myself repeating: unless she wasn't there at all.

You might think that these were idle musings, but I assure you there was nothing idle about them. I thought very actively and consistently about my neighbors, and hated them for it. I spied on them from my window. I listened for the sounds of their lives. I rifled through their mail, left on the common hall table by Esther the postwoman, to ensure, I told myself, that a Mrs. Wandor did indeed exist at our address. One such did receive correspondence, although not very much: she subscribed to the *Radio Times*, and the electric and gas bills came for her. But it wouldn't have been difficult, I knew, for these supposed proofs to have been addressed to a phantom. There did not need to be a Mrs. Wandor in order for the *Radio Times* to arrive in her name: it might, I told myself, be just a canny ruse.

I had become a voyeur, the hunted a hunter. I blamed Ridley Wandor: she had invaded my little life just as I had known she would. Just as she had intended. Do not think, as I knew not to think, that this was anything other than Ridley Wandor's own plan. This was what she had wanted.

One night, when I got up to go to the bathroom well before dawn, I made, in my spying, a further discovery, whose import was unclear. In that room, doubtless on account of the water pipes, although perhaps because of the ever-open window, noise traveled much more clearly from their plane to mine; and as I

stood, preparing to flush, I was stopped by stumbling, by sob-
bing, by violent retching. It was, though somewhat muffled,
very near: I shared the *intimité* of the Wandor water closet.
Aghast, I was also transfixed. Riveted. The wrenching racket
went on, and on, in spite of the fact that the ailing one, or her
carer, turned on the taps, perhaps to drown the noise. Sobs,
retching, running water, then murmurs, almost mutters—but
whose voice? and saying what? I waited a long time, or what
seemed, to my moonlit nakedness, a long time, without moving
or flushing, not wanting them, thereby, to know that I was overhead. But I could not wait long enough: eventually, shivering although it was the height of summer, I tiptoed away, the toilet
unflushed, while the commotion continued beneath me.

Would you say that I grew too involved in the lives of my
neighbors? Or rather, that they foisted themselves too vigorously upon me? Lest you leap, too swiftly, to the former conclusion, let me tell you this: the day after the aural assault in my
bathroom, I was sorely tempted, at last, to ring the Wandor
doorbell on my way out to the library, the way my own doorbell
had been rung several weeks before. I knew that it would be a
further invitation to the insidious titterer, and I wanted nothing less than to have to look upon her again; but I had devel-
oped, by then, a great fear for Mrs. Wandor, whom I now
imagined dosed on arsenic or some marginally less violent
emetic, enfeebled but not allowed simply to die. For what reasons? Perversity, pure and simple, seemed perhaps a contribut-
ing, but surely not a catalytic factor. No, I imagined that a
small—or even substantial—pension or annuity was at stake,
that Mrs. Wandor was medically controlled by her daughter the

way decrepit popes or Soviet potentates of yore were propped up, dull-eyed, to placate the masses, while their scheming advisors, eminences grises, held the reins behind them, in order that the pair might keep their flat, their rabbits, their petty luxuries. Yes, in her bland—deceptively bland—and hulking exterior, with her false bonhomie, Ridley Wandor was most certainly an eminence grise.

I was kept from my half-formed plan to save the old lady— because what was behind my will to intervene? not, surely, perversity pure and simple; but rather, I believe, a thread of samaritanism that dwells still in me in spite of all the brutal disappointments I have suffered—anyway, as I was saying, I was prevented from ringing that doorbell that morning by a ringing of my own—unexpected, uninvited and, given that I had made no provision for it, inescapable. For the first time in my sojourn, the telephone rang. Promptly at 8:30, as I sat at the splendid, companionable kitchen table with, before me, a steaming *Tasse* of coffee and my secret vice, *The Daily Mail*, the high-pitched jangling erupted. Unlike the front doorbell, which I had tested, the phone was unknown to me (it is not easy to telephone oneself by way of experiment), and I let out a little cry, in conjunction with which my hand spasmed, jerking the *tasse* and sending coffee all over the pulpy newsprint in a sodden mash. My morning was ruined.

The caller was a colleague of mine, a classicist, a man whose own summer peregrinations had taken him to Umbria— not, so far as I could tell, in the interests of research, but rather in pursuit of a glamour he could never truly hope to attain. He was a small, round-headed fellow, clownishly bald, whose large, damp, dark eyes were framed by extravagant lashes. He had a high, nasal voice, considerable, if unkind, wit, and an extraordinary memory. He could recite details of ancient faculty meetings with absolute authority; could revivify conversations held at dinner parties a decade before, complete with a list of the foods and drinks consumed, and by whom they had been consumed. He could recall the year, the month, and even the day of the week upon which such a dinner party had taken place. I have no definite evidence that he was able to apply this extraordinary skill to his scholarship, and am inclined to think that even if he was, it served him but little, as he proved no more able than I to propel himself from our comfortable minor undergraduate institution, in its minor town, in its minor corner of New England: he had already been there, at that point, for eighteen years. Whereas I was still striving, he had renounced, and claimed himself happy with his lot. In compensation for irrelevance, he treated himself to luxurious holidays, such as this month in Umbria—in a hillside farmhouse near Spoleto, through which had passed, I conjectured, a flurry of handsome young men, some former students, some truck drivers or gardeners, all sculpted and bronzed, mop-headed and witless, the antitheses of their brilliant but pale and clammy host. He was discreet, for the most part, in his amorous delvings; but on several past occasions, his persistence had outstripped his discretion. He had been warned, and now knew to conduct his passions not only out of term, but out of the country. It was an arrangement seemingly suitable to all.

Done with his frolics, this professor, whose name was Richard Copley, was stopping in London on his way home. His extraordinary memory had tipped him to my presence in that city of ten million, and his wit, or his persistence, had tracked me. It wasn't, in fact, so difficult: he had merely called my department secretary, a breathy recent graduate named Camelia, whose entanglement with the lacrosse coach had kept her in town, and she had furnished him with my London number, e-mailed to that office by me "in case of emergency."

"How's Doctor Death, then?" was his opening jest. I have not mentioned—it had not seemed germane—that the topic of my research that summer was, indeed, death, an analysis of the shift between an eighteenth-century conception of death and a Romantic conception thereof, and ultimately of the poetic manifestations of that shift. In London, though, I was engaged in the practical preliminaries of this project, the pre-literary aspects: I was tracing, or trying to trace, demographic changes in the means of death during the relevant periods. I was looking at how the general populace, in London in partic-ular, had died in those times. Or rather, if precision is my aim, at how they were said to have died, as "grief" and "old age" were two too-frequent ascriptions of the cause. I had long been looking forward to writing this book, which I was determined would be my "breakthrough" text; although, in truth, I had thought the same, and misguidedly, about my first volume, *Date with Destiny?*, which examined the life and work of those ill-fated 1950s American poets, to attempt to determine whether they prescribed their deaths or were proscribed by them. Most academics have a period—the Renaissance; Romanticism; the Moderns—but some of us, the newer models, have a subject rather than a time. We find it more exhilarating, less constraining. My subject, undeniably, was—it is—death; hence the sobriquet, which I shared with Kevorkian, the euthanasia dervish of that moment, whose mission is at least in part the focus of my next endeavor, *Defying Death, Denying God: The Kirilov Principle,* and so he was, perhaps, an obvious bedfellow.

"How's Doctor Death, then?" Copley said to me, straight off, with a whinnying snigger. Still startled by the phone's ring, I could not immediately place the voice, the jest, the snigger, and so said nothing. Indeed, my first thought was that Ridley Wandor, to whom the nickname might more aptly have been given, was calling to torment me with what she knew I knew.

"It's Copley, you fool," he continued into the silence. "Beelzebub got your tongue?"

"Copley. Of course."

"I'm in Soho," he said. "Blowing my year's salary on a literary treat. Hazlitt's. Know it?"

"I know where it is."

"Shabby chic. Very London. How about lunch?"

"I don't know, Richard—"

"It's Dick to you. Don't want your workday disrupted, eh? Nosing too deep in the mire? I always remember that about you—very particular in your work habits."

"I suppose, Richard—"

"Dick, I tell you. Supper then? How about somewhere near you? Let me see your pad?"

"It's not much of a neighborhood for restaurants."

"Where are you?"

I wavered, pondering Sheila Cooke's lie; then decided that honesty, in this instance, might suffice to repel him. "Kilburn," I said.

"Where's that?"

"Beyond Maida Vale; far beyond Little Venice. It's Irish, and immigrants. No charm."

"The charm of the real city," he said, with a further snigger. "I've got a weakness for those Irish laborers, the young boys with the freckles. The Catholics."

"Please, Richard."

"We can eat at a pub. Or a curry in a hurry—isn't that what they say? The local Indian? Tell me how to get to you. I'll be there at seven-thirty."

So discombobulated was I by this interruption of my privacy, so frazzled at the prospect of Copley plumply installed in my sitting room, that I rushed through my ablutions and out the door, hoping to retrieve, in the quiet of the library, some modicum of peace. I quite forgot about the Wandors, mother and daughter: their mutual torture, if such it was, and their torture of me, evaporated, at least temporarily, in the face of this all-too-real diversion.

Copley was, as ever, prompt. I'd laid my hands on a succulent but light Brouilly, some Spanish olives and bakery cheese straws, only by cutting short my working day and making the considerable detour to Swiss Cottage on my way home: Kilburn did not run to cheese straws. And although I knew—I knew Copley well enough to know—that my guest, in forcing himself upon me in this way was secretly hoping that I would cook for him (they always hope for it, those guests who have had the privilege before), I had decided that his intrusion could not go unpunished. If he claimed to want to eat at a restaurant in my neck of the woods, then in my neck of the woods we would dine, with all its attendant horrors. I had, that afternoon, troubled to make a booking at the New Kilburn Tandoori, that grim establishment whose faded velvet drapes and smeared windows had, upon my first visit to the neighborhood, somehow eluded my scrutiny. The man at the end of the line, whose accent was charmingly pronounced, made no effort to disguise his astonishment: "But I beg your pardon," he said, "it really is not necessary."

"Are you in possession of a little plastic placard that reads 'Reserved'?"

"But of course. Quite naturally. But you see—"

"Then please put it on a table set for two. On one of the tables in the window. So that we can see the world passing by."

"Very good, then. As you wish. In what name? Yes, no problem. See you at half past eight."

I had allotted, then, an hour for drinks with Copley, knowing full well he would be prompt. It seemed the civilized gesture; but I was aware, too, of its masochism. He, rounder than ever, a veritable little Bibendum, and freckled by the Italian sun, blinked his deep eyes furiously when I opened the door, spread his arms wide and cried, "My dear! My dear!" in high campery. I stepped gingerly into his embrace, and stiffened there, allowing him to plant a moist kiss near my right ear.

"Divine!" he said. "Simply divine to see you, *out of context,* my dear creature. Let me in, let me in—I must know how you've been living."

"Must you, Richard? Why?"

He stopped in the kitchen, lifted his fleshy nose, flared, and sniffed. The cheese straws were warming in the oven and had perfumed the entire flat.

"I'm not feeding you, I'm afraid," I said. "You wanted local color."

"Of course I did, my dear. Of course. What a view—a voyeur's paradise! I love it." He had wandered to the window, from which, although it was still light outside, one could see all the animated figurines in the houses opposite busily acting and reacting.

"They can see us just the same," I reminded him.

"Only they aren't looking, are they, my dear?" He rubbed his hands together with glee. "Too busy feeding and flossing and fucking to look out of their windows, wouldn't you say?"

I shrugged.

"Besides which, if my memory serves, you're here alone, in the end. Isn't that so?"

I busied myself with the cheese straws. The flat was furnished with a set of oven mitts adorned with the heads of famous composers: they were a routine source of amusement for me, but I did not, at that moment, point them out to my guest.

"My point being merely, my dear, that your life is wholly blameless. Even were they to look. Isn't it so?"

I made a noncommittal noise in the back of my throat, and feigned great preoccupation with the transfer of the cheese straws to the cabbage-leaf bowl.

"Not like me, eh?" He whinnied, and in his laugh I caught a timbre of the Wandor titter, a timbre that made me wheel around and look, just to be sure it was in fact Copley in my kitchen. "You know me, my dear. A terrible old goat. Don't know how you do it, but I'd love to have your restraint."

"Blame Catullus. I don't spend my time with those over-stimulating ancients, Richard. That must be the secret."

He twinkled, bit the end off a steaming cheese straw, and marched towards the sitting room. "Let's sit. Let's drink. Let's have a chat, my dear," he called over his fleshy shoulder. "Didn't I spy a tasty red on that divine kitchen table of yours? That table alone is worth the rent. What do you pay, by the way?"

I had no intention of telling Copley my rent, any more than he would reveal to me the exorbitant sums he had forked over for his den of Italian iniquity. There was a great deal I did not wish to discuss with Copley, but which he seemed determined to winkle out of me; and in that dangerous hour of wine without food—for when there is food before one there is always, somehow, something to say—I found my usually formidable powers of deflection sorely tested. I am not, in general, someone who finds reserve difficult; and yet, I am not, generally, someone who would allow so endlessly appetitive a figure as Copley to converse, untrammeled, with myself alone, in my sitting room. Rest assured, I did not speak about those matters I did not wish to discuss; but I did find myself forced to speak. And it was Ridley Wandor who filled the gap.

It was strange how this oblique suet of a woman emerged, in my description, as a figure of near-gothic luridness. It was perhaps in part that I sought—through hyperbole, the trope of our age—to entertain my malicious guest; but it was not solely that. I did not manufacture, on Copley's account, a morbid fascination; I merely revealed a fascination already extant, and one which, as it aired and filled the room around us, proved every bit as private, and hence shameful to discuss, as would have been the aspects of my personal life I was going to such lengths to avoid. Shame: yes. I felt ashamed to have revealed to this untrustworthy companion that I had given so much attention, and even thought, to the comings and goings of the Wandor household. In my defense, I pointed out that my actions were, in fact, *reactions*; that I was by no means the instigator of this curious relationship.

"What relationship?" Copley needled. "The woman introduced herself, to be neighborly. You ran into her on the High Road. Once. This is all in your head, my dear. All in your head."

"But you don't understand—they—or at least, she, because I'm not wholly convinced that there is a *they*, she'd been spying on me. She knew I was alone—she—"

"Everyone"—he gestured at the houses opposite, now bright as stage sets—"every last one who cares to know knows that you're alone. That in itself doesn't make you a victim, you know."

I did not reply. I sniffed my Brouilly.

"Although I know it might feel that way. You need to get used to it, the solitude. Myself, you know, I only really feel alive this way," he continued, an unhealthy zest illuminating his large eyes. "The boys, the buggery—it's like combing my hair, or eating breakfast. It's—no, it's more like a good shit. Satisfying, necessary, but once it's done—what relevance does it have to who I am, to what I experience in a day? Very little. It's a given. A physical requirement. But it only reinforces my individual integrity, if you see what I mean." He paused. I blinked, which he took as an invitation to expand further. "If I gave away a portion of that integrity to someone else—*well*. I'd feel less myself, not more. I'd feel less *alive*. But I don't think we're alike in this, my friend, are we?"

I looked at my watch. "Eight-thirty," I said. "We have a reservation."

"My sense is that left alone, far from feeling more fully alive, Doctor Death feels that little bit closer to death. Is that possible?"

"Suppertime, Richard."

He narrowed his eyes; the extensive lashes appeared to entangle before them, so it was as if he peered at me through a thicket. "Is that even a little desirable, my dear? Or more than a little?"

"The last cheese straw, Richard?"

"My dear."

It was only a block and a half in the dusk. A clutch of children were out playing on the neighbors' front patch, watched from the doorway by a Middle Eastern woman whose swarthy face and hands were all that emerged from her swaddling. Across the street, in front of the flats I now knew to be public housing, three muscled youths bared their torsos to the passers-by and pretended to work on their car, a rusted blue Vauxhall with a dent in the side and the hood up. Signs were alight on the High Road, but the shops and stalls were closed for the day, and the thoroughfare had assumed, in spite of the traffic, its desolate night aspect: wavering papers, gummed to the pavement by unnameable effluvia, fluttered under the gassy streetlamps. The gutters flowed with peel and rubbish. The pubs—three were in view from the intersection of my street with the High Road—emitted inviting rumblings from behind their galleon-fronted, frosted-window facades.

"If you're really after an Irish boy," I said, pointing northwards, "you'll want to have a crawl through the joints up that way."

"You wouldn't come along, would you?"

I smiled.

"Ah, well. Didn't think so. No, let's have supper, then, instead. What's it to be?"

Copley's clownish face fell at the sight of the New Kilburn Tandoori. I fleetingly felt something akin to regret for my perversity, and had half a mind to offer fried eggs on toast at my flat instead. But then I recalled his needling, and my shame. I recalled the bumptious disregard of his morning telephone call, the determination with which he had foisted himself upon me. And I thought of the panic I would feel were he to cross my threshold again, the threat of indefinite interruption: from the restaurant, the path back to his extravagant hotel was clearly outlined, whereas, were he to come back into my home, to settle his plump bottom at my splendid table, then there might be no way to uproot him.

"Curry in a hurry," I ventured, as I drew the door wide for him, and pushed back a panel of velveteen drape. "Just what you hoped for, I believe?"

The food, let it be said, was less vile than we might have anticipated. Certainly, it was not sufficiently unpalatable to explain the ratio of employees to customers, which stood at two to one: besides ourselves, there was only one single man installed in a dark corner, violently slurping at his sauce-filled plate. The dinner did suffer from a surfeit of what, in India, might actually have been ghee, but which was, in North London, simply vegetable oil; and its flavors were rather more insipid than one might have wished; but all in all its acceptability, so unexpected, provided fodder for our flagging conversation, and led us, quite naturally, to a discussion of other cuisines, and, in light of Copley's recent junket, to Italian food at its lower levels. He saluted the cheer of a peasant cuisine such as Umbria's, which ensures that the finest practitioners need not come from the grandest of homes.

I put Copley in a minicab shortly after ten-thirty: Kilburn did not run to black cabs, at that inconvenient hour. No doubt, so close to the closing hour of those infamous pubs, the cabbies steered well clear of the area. Anyway, Copley squeezed into the back of some small, stained vehicle, powerfully scented of lemon disinfectant and hair oil, driven by a young African in a loudly striped red-and-green sweater. My colleague pressed my hand with his chubby fingers, after he had sunk, pasha-like, into his ill-sprung seat.

"You take care, my dear. I don't like what I see. It worries me."

I laughed.

"Not enough of that, I'm thinking. Beware of that woman's rabbits. They may seem harmless, but they're a vicious species." He blinked at me coyly, and stifled a soft belch. "The Indian's repeating on me. Better head back to my downy bed."

"It's early yet—in Soho, I imagine—"

"Might get a second wind. As it were. You're quite right, I just might. Depends on the pickings and, quite frankly, on the price. For God's sake, my dear, what are you doing out here, when you could be at the heart of things? You're a very queer fish indeed."

I shut the door on him and watched them go, down the High Road to Maida Vale and beyond. I felt both sorrow and relief: Copley was right, quite right, to deduce that I felt less alive—immediately less alive, as though all past and any possible future melted away the moment his taxi rounded the bend, leaving me, a quavering atom of the present, in the vast cosmic void of Kilburn. But my soul's retreat, when thus shucked of all attributes and aspirations, was—and is—into a sort of somnambulism, an affectless and almost restful state. A functional version of suspended animation, to be feared and courted in equal measure. As I walked the little distance home, I was a purified and passive entity: aware of the rustling leaves, the distant hoots and calls of drunken youth on their way home, buffeted by the various odors, of garbage and greenery and cooling asphalt, bathed by the evening's intermittent breeze. But I had not a thought beyond these receptors: drained by the efforts of expression and repression, far from the prospect of the morrow (another long and dreary library day, another solitary supper; which would lead, in turn, to merely another lonely night, sweating in my moonlit bed, and thence to still further days and dinners without end—a rolling future of futility the contemplation of which made death glow like home), I merely ambled. I was almost loath to go in; but the decision to keep strolling through the deserted streets required more than I could muster. I crossed the threshold like a child told by his mother to come in after play, dragging my heels but resigned.

Ultimately, though, Copley's visit was not good for me. This is an understatement. That simple, single evening—for if Copley stayed any longer in London, I was unaware of it—wreaked havoc on my state of mind. In order to make the most of my London summer, I had carefully stowed my sorrows in a locked box: my lost love; the endlessly lonely life that awaited me upon my Labor Day return; the professional frustrations with which I grappled, and the striving, apparently fruitless, for recognition by my peers; the ailing older brother in Maine— obese, mind you, and with no one to blame for his condition but himself—to whom I was not at all close but whose condition periodically preoccupied me out of guilt; and, most glaringly, the grotesque futility of it all, of which my brother's obesity seemed but one of many logical manifestations—all this, I had padlocked safely in a sequestered trunk, the lock to which Copley, who nosed it out immediately and uninvited, had spent hours picking. He had assaulted my solitude. Put otherwise, it was as if he had taken away my anesthetic, and my wounds ached horribly. And what—he was quite right to marvel at it, in his round and freckled smugness—what on earth was I doing, in that sunlit but unremarkable flat, in that drab corner of what I knew full well to be Kilburn, leading a non-life at London's periphery when I ought to have been seizing the pulsing variety at its core? And then, another voice within would counter: What pleasures would there be, therein, for you? For Copley, perhaps, with his physical needs and un-abashed gluttony—but for you? Then spoke reason, in its turn: the aim of this summer was thoroughly to research the histori-cal data—those endless, pointless, delicious deaths—for my book. The rest was flimflam, vanities. And the demon again: Were not those very deaths vanities themselves? For what, for whom, this striving, if not for myself who had ceased to care?

It is not necessary to lay out here, in full, the endless inter-nal debates in which I indulged: the point is that on the morn-ing after my supper with Copley, I got up and dressed and breakfasted, but could not drag myself to the bus stop for my trip to the library. I sat instead on my living room sofa, orga-nizing notecards, telling myself it was a necessary day of rest and regeneration. The following day, my only sortie was to Marks and Spencer to replenish my stocks, and although I pretended to sort my notecards, I spent long hours staring out the window at the movements of toylike people whose comical little lives appeared a good bit more urgent than my own. (It should be noted that in the afternoons, before the lights were lit that so obligingly revealed the interiors opposite, I had only gardens to gaze upon; and that these were largely undisturbed by human-ity. So that I alone tracked the scamperings of squirrels, the sly insinuations of the local tabby cats, and the black mutt's miser-able battle with his chain.) On the third day, I did not get out of bed at all, except, of course, for necessary trips to the bathroom. I took books to bed with me, but I did not read them. I had lost interest, too, in my food, usually so important to me, and consumed only a single Marks and Spencer platter in a day; although on that third day, in my indifference, I allowed the dish to burn, indeed to char—the smoke, when I opened the oven, billowed impressively—and so I ate nothing at all.

The scent of near-fire, however, had another effect: seeping out of my flat and spreading through the common hallway below, it attracted the attention of Ridley Wandor. When, that evening after dark, I heard the infernal doorbell, I knew at once that it heralded the return of my forgotten nemesis—because she *had* been forgotten, she and her mother: in my three days of confinement, my aimless reveries had taken me far, far from the quotidian round of our shared home—and I contemplated not answering. But there were lights on in my flat; they could be seen from the landing. And if she, or her mother, had been at home, they would certainly have heard my periodic tread, from the bedroom to the bathroom and back again. You may say that I wanted, really, to open the door: I absolutely did not. But I felt I had no choice. In my robe and slippers, at nine o'clock at night, I stood disheveled before Ridley Wandor.

For the first time in my memory, she was not wearing a shell suit. Instead, she sported a silky black T-shirt, a dressy sort of garment that reflected, almost, across her breasts, and a pilled scarlet blazer with unfashionably wide lapels (so unfashionable, indeed, that they approached the latest retro style). These colors only highlighted the pallor of her skin, the mousiness of her hair. She bore a recent long scratch along the jut of her imposing chin, the scab of which was red. I stared at it, and fiddled with the belt of my robe.

"I hope it's not too late," she began, with her inimitable chilling laugh. "You're not in bed already, are you? There were lights on, or I would never . . ."

"It's fine," I said. "I'm just a little under the weather. What may I do for you?"

"Under the weather! I knew it! We've been worried about you, Mother and me. Quiet as a church mouse up here. And then, you didn't pick up your post today"—she held out a couple of flyers of no interest, and a bill—"and then, of course, the terrible smell this afternoon. And I said to myself, It's time, Ridley, it's time to look in upstairs and make sure everything's all right."

"Very thoughtful of you. Yes, no, it's all just fine. I'd invite you in, but as you can see—"

"Oh, I don't mind *that*!" She referred to my bathrobe. "I'm a very casual person, myself. Now Mother, she's more formal, more traditional, really. But nothing flaps me. I'm caring for the aged, mind, and that's right down to wiping their bums, if you'll pardon me saying so." She stepped forward, forcing me to step back. She had entered my flat. "You don't have anyone to help out, do you?"

"I haven't needed anyone." I detected a distinct hamsterly smell emanating from her person, which puzzled me only until I remembered the rabbits. Those powerful rabbits might also explain, I thought, the scratch: after all, it was either the rabbits or, more troublingly, the mother.

"Shall I fix you a cup of tea?" she asked, moving towards

the kettle with a forthright confidence. My face must have betrayed my surprise, because she stopped, and tittered. "Do you forget that this is what I do? You're under the weather; let Ridley take care of you."

"No, please. I feel—"

"Peaky. You look frankly peaky. That's what my mother would say. You probably haven't been eating properly, have you?"

I spluttered, panicked; to no avail.

"I'll fix you some lovely toast and jam. You just sit, sit down at that lovely table. It's the one thing that was old Eric's, I think. The one and only thing."

"Eric?"

"He was the sitting tenant, don't you know. The *other* sitting tenant, because Mother and me, we're sitting tenants too, of course."

"I see."

"I doubt you do, do you? Do you have sitting tenants in America?"

"I don't know."

She laughed her wince-making laugh. "You don't *know?*"

I was silent.

"Eric, like Mum and me, had lived here a long time. He'd lived here longer. Since the seventies, I reckon. Funny old duck. He lived here with his wife, till she passed—we never knew her—and then he lived here on his own. Then he had a fall, poor chap, and he wasn't ever quite the same after, though he lived on another four or five years. And he didn't have any family, did he? So I stopped in on him, every day by the end. And when it was the last couple of weeks I'd sit up with him some nights, although Mother didn't like it—she'd hit the ceiling with the broomstick to tell me to come home, but I just told old Eric it was the bunnies thumping around." She paused to rummage in my small refrigerator for butter, milk, jam. I sat as if paralyzed at the table, my hands spread flat over its scored wood. It was a grave blow to me to learn that this table had not come from a companionable home, but rather had sat alone, for years, with a dying man. I was suddenly aware—it was almost a physical pain, a tightening along my rib cage—that Sheila Cooke had lured me into a house of death. I had been fooled by the sunlight, by the emphatic wealth of life in the buildings opposite. But I saw now that this was a station outside life; like the rampart of a medieval town, it was a place from which to observe, a defense and a trap.

Ridley Wandor was speaking again: "—he's an Indian fellow—there are so many in this neighborhood now—"

"I'm sorry. Eric?"

"No, no. Not Eric. He was from Huddersfield, originally. No, the landlord. Taha. Mr. Taha. Who bought the building from O'Leary, the couple that owned it before. They're the ones broke it up into flats. O'Leary was a contractor, and they moved up in the world, crossed over to West Hampstead, if you please. They owned several places along this road—regular slumlords. Rachman types. But you don't know about him either, do you?"

I raised my eyebrows. It was the only gesture I could muster.

"He's neither here nor there. I was telling you about Taha. Mr. Taha, the fellow who bought from the O'Learys—cheap, too, because of us lot—"

"I'm sorry?"

"The sitting tenants. That's the point. He can't get rid of us, and he can't unreasonably raise the rent. We have rights. He has to wait for us to die—he's probably willing us to die—so that he can do what he did here."

"Here?"

"With Eric's flat—I mean, your flat."

"Just for the summer."

"Well, you see. He gutted the place, except for Eric's old table, and gussied it up, and now—how much are you paying?"

I stared at my hands, spread out on the table, as if their veins were a source of great fascination. Still paralyzed, I was growing hot within my skin, and I feared that my wrath might show.

"Of course, forgive me. It's a rude question. Now, here's your tea"—she plunked a large milky mug before me—"and some toast. You only had marmalade, so marmalade it is. Shall I pop another slice in the toaster straightaway?"

I longed for the telephone to ring, but knew it would not.

"I'm just rambling, anyway, it's not about how much you pay, it's about a change, you see, a change in the community. If they're all as very nice as you are—"

"They?"

"The tenants who come after. And the ones he'll put in upstairs, someday. It's very strange, that: it's been empty for the three years since he bought the place. I heard he was saving it for someone in the family—a mother, a brother, something, coming over from India. But they don't ever come, do they?"

I ate my toast. It required, or seemed to, a great deal of chewing, slow and bovine. I burned my tongue on the tea.

"We've stopped wondering. This place was three or four

months empty before you came. I told Mother that Taha must be asking too much."

A crumb caught in my throat.

"Are you all right?" She reached as if to pat my back, and I put my hands up to ward her off.

"Trust me," she said, although she backed away. "I take care of people."

When I had recovered, I spoke. I tried to do so authoritatively, but without revealing my rage or repulsion. "Miss Wandor—"

"Ridley, please. You make me feel like my *mother*."

I nodded. I would not say it. "Yes, well, I'm so very grateful for your thoughtful visit, and for the toast and tea—most restorative—but I'm not feeling entirely well, and I think I'd better be getting back to bed."

She stood, and squared her shoulders, tightening the shiny shirt across her bulk. "Of course you should. A good night's rest and you'll be right as rain tomorrow."

I, too, stood, and shepherded her towards the door, my arms crossed to hold in my rage.

"Don't worry, you won't die," she said in the doorway, with a titter.

"I beg your pardon?"

"I think some people think, you know, because of what I do—"

"The caring business."

"Yes, exactly. But because they all do—they all do die, you see . . . I think some people think, or might think, that it's a bad omen to have me take care of them."

"Who are those people, Miss Wandor, who would think that?"

"I don't know." She blushed. It was quite extraordinary to behold, a hot pink wash across the vast insipid planes of her face. Even the scratch on her chin seemed more full of blood. "I just don't want you to think it. To worry about it."

"Of course not."

She did not move, stood hulking there. Then whispered, "It's just that—lately—they die faster."

"I'm sorry?"

"Every time I go, they die within weeks. Seven. Three. Five. That's the last three. It used to be months, even years." She was quite red now: even her puffy hands looked flushed, as they grasped at my door, one on the knob as if to open it, the other pressing on the wood as if to keep it shut. Her words tumbled in an embarrassed huddle. "I know it isn't my fault. It can't be. But each time, I've had thoughts, you know how it is, or you can see how it must be—they're very weak, and often very bad-tempered—it's uncomfortable for them—great age is a curse—and they whine, or they rail at me, or they wet the bed for the third time in a day, and I don't say—of course I don't"—she tittered, anxiously—"but you can't help but think it, can you? And each time, it happens, it just follows on: I've thought it, I've wished it, and it happens. Doesn't it? It's as if I had a power—"

"Please, Miss Wandor—surely you don't believe—"

"And I can't tell Mother—you have to understand. I wouldn't have said anything, but who else can I tell? And you've been so pleasant, I feel we're friends, really—new friends, of course, but—"

"Miss Wandor, you seem quite distraught. I can't think—"

"But you have to understand, I can't tell Mother." Tears welled up in her little eyes. "Because in a way, I take care of her, too. Don't I?"

"I suppose you do."

"And we have our differences, and thoughts—well, they come without permission, don't they?"

I said nothing.

"Tell me, it isn't just me, is it? I can't seem to control my thoughts, but then—"

"You're overly superstitious, Miss Wandor. Truly you are." I almost reached out to put my hand on her shoulder, but I quashed the impulse, too repelled by her quivers. "The world doesn't work that way, I'm afraid. If it did, our thoughts could *save* lives, and as I'm sure you've realized, they can't."

"Maybe someone's can?" Ridley Wandor paused in her frank crying to ponder the notion, then redoubled her tears. "But not mine. Because I just bring death, wherever I go."

"I think you need some rest, more even than I do," I said. "You're overwrought. It comes from working with the dying; a very noble and challenging calling, I'm sure, but doubtless disturbing, too. You must need a vacation. A holiday, as you call it here. That's all. You should speak to your doctor. Tomorrow. Trust me. Go to sleep now, and put these silly ideas out of your head. Thoughts don't kill people."

She snuffled, squinted at me. "You don't think so?"

"I know so. Miss Wandor, I'm quite certain of it. You have absolutely nothing to worry about. Now, I thank you for the tea and toast, and I thank you for the kindness of looking in on me, but please—" I was quite firm. "You must go home to your mother. She'll be wondering where you are."

Meekly, like a child, she bowed her head and opened the door; but had barely crossed the threshold when she turned again. "I start a new one tomorrow. An old fellow who lives with his daughter. I don't know, I don't have a good feeling about it."

"Everything will be just fine. You mustn't worry. It's natural. It's in the course of things..." I stopped, and took a breath. "Please, Miss Wandor. Go home."

If Copley's intrusion had ruptured my routines and halted my momentum, Ridley Wandor's outburst unsettled me in quite another way. It enervated me—this is perhaps the most apt description I can provide. I washed the mug, the plate—most vigorously, because I feared, irrationally, that she carried with her some microbial taint—and, turning off all the lights, retreated to my bed. But I could not sleep. I had not been sleeping before, any more than I had been working: I had been lying in bed, in the night's blue luminescence, feeling drained, and vague and milky. It had been a type of despair, I suppose: a near-catatonia. I had been careful not to think of my lost love and my failed life, had been willfully repressing the cloud of my terrible aloneness; and so had been left in the same state as a boat becalmed in fog: unseeing, unmoving, unmoored.

But Ridley Wandor's interlude had thoroughly changed my

temper. As I lay again between the same rumpled sheets, which had retained a trace of their earlier warmth; as the night's secret light pooled and shadowed in the room around me, I found my heart and breathing thrumming in syncopated haste, and my ears straining, aching to hear. I feared what she might do. I feared what she had meant.

Hers was an absurd outburst—a part of me knew that to be so, and willed my trembling fingers to still; but it seemed that too much of my battered psyche had fallen prey to her machinations—because machinations I was certain they were—and the trembling did not stop. My terrors were both natural and supernatural, if you will; and although I recognized the madness of them altogether, they whizzed around my brain unheeding and caused small explosions of light behind my eyes. For one thing, I panicked that from behind her veil of crocodile tears, my neighbor had in fact been confessing. Had she not told me that her patients were dying before her eyes and, essentially, at her hands? She had couched the gruesome facts in eerie hypotheticals—as if it were her thoughts, rather than her puffy hands, that perpetrated the acts—but was it not, perhaps, a cry for help from a woman pervaded by evil? Or even, more simply still, a very sick woman indeed; which I knew her, had known her from first sight, to be? This was a common phenomenon, in the "caring business," her membership in which she so vaunted: nurses of various types routinely smothered their charges; or overdosed their IVs; or injected their collapsing veins; or still, less aggressively but no less culpably, stood by doing nothing in the face of an attack, when so little—a pill, a shot, who knew, a slap?—might retrieve the dying patient from death's jaws. It was common among nurses, even doctors, not merely in America but in genteel Britain, too, as I well knew from my secret readings of *The Daily Mail*. I even knew what it was called—I say "even," but of course it was my duty to know, my very livelihood, that livelihood being death. Munchausen's Syndrome By Proxy. Munchausen's Syndrome being, of course, a disorder wherein the patient commits harm against himself, undergoes unnecessary medical procedures, for example, simply in order to attract a certain type of attention. And those tiny words—"by proxy"—exist to deepen, exponentially, the ultimate gravity of the disorder: because instead of harm to self, the patient does harm to others. The patient, let it be said, ultimately wants to be caught. And what, then, was Ridley Wandor's inappropriate outburst but a murderer's plea to be stopped? She *had* killed, she had as much as said so; she had killed at least three of her patients, and was worried that she might kill a fourth. She was worried—just as I had indeed worried—that she might, in fact, turn her dastardly hand against her mother. She had admitted outright that the thought had crossed her mind. Just as I had predicted, just as I had thought—only I had thought the deed already long done, and in that sense my thoughts were premonitory, even clairvoyant— my downstairs neighbor was, or would be, responsible for her mother's untimely death.

And yet. And yet. I was not so far detached from reality as not to see the practical unlikelihood of this reading of events. Not least because I could not imagine the scenario in which I would step forward and speak either to the police, or to the agency for which she worked, nor even, perhaps most of all, to Mrs. Wandor, whose life I construed to be in danger. It was not possible that these scenes would or could take place; nor was it possible for me to imagine, in the wake of a bloody bludgeoning beneath me, my own self dumbly gawping and shouldering the guilt—"But I knew! But she told me! And if only I had acted . . ." No: I could not see it; such things did not happen.

And yet. The other eventuality, the supernatural, which might on one level have seemed still more outlandish, seemed yet somehow easier to accept: that she was not veiling her truth, but rather telling it, to the best of her ability; that she did wish her patients dead, and that they did, subsequently, die; just as I, by thinking so long upon it, had wished intrigue into the flat below, only to have it climb the stairs and visit me, ostensibly uninvited, but in fact willed, willed for weeks. I had wanted to know what was going on, and now I knew. She had wanted those patients to die, and now they had.

Think of it, in other contexts: sexual attraction, for instance. Do we not will it to be mutual, and are our wishes not, more often than not, fulfilled? Or success: do we not, as countless preaching capitalists insist over our television screens or on our radios, attract only as much wealth and power as we will, with our most concentrated minds, towards us? And there are those who argue the same of health, to be sure: who see in every polyp, every tumor, every chromosomal mischance, some active failure of thought, of will, on the part of the stricken. Why not, then, death? Why could it not be willed upon another—without meaning to, without lifting a finger? It was, as a notion, but a tiny step from the others, no less, if no more, logical.

And then the round and corpulent Copley loomed before me, insisting, in his waggish way, that my solitude, unlike his own, brought me only closer to death. Was this what he had unwittingly meant: that Death herself, so poorly disguised, would climb my staircase and weep on my threshold? That was nonsense: what he had meant was that I slowed, hibernant, in isolation, and that my morbid imagination turned the cemetery soil like any professional gravedigger. And what was I doing, wriggling in my wrinkled sheets in the slowly passing night, if not that?

After it was all over, I felt the terrible inadequacy of the premonitory powers I had simultaneously feared and gloated over in myself. What transpired took a long time, so long indeed that were it not for my own ghoulish curiosity, my need, long after I had left the sun-filled flat in Kilburn that I came to think of, after that night, as old Eric's, and deadly, to test my own imagination, my narrative will, if you like, against the facts; were it not, that is to say, for my certainty that I had imagined, and thereby willed, the story exactly as it must play out, I wouldn't have inquired and so never would have known. By that time, I was far away in New England, at a great remove of time and space from the Wandors altogether, and even from *The Daily Mail*, which would, had I but seen it, have apprised me of the details.

By that time, spring, less than a year later—but how long those months can be, as well as how short, and what distances

I had myself traveled in that time—I was back in my niche at the college. And yet, in some other way, was thoroughly unnested. For the better, I might add. I had met someone new—or rather, had met again someone whom I had previously, if only vaguely, known, in a different context and in a different way—and this person, to my terror and surprise, had changed me. Or had met a changed me. We were living together (as we continue to do), not where I had long lived, in a purpose-built bachelor flat in a low brick building in that small college town, but in Boston, a couple of hours away, in a high-ceilinged apartment in a brownstone we had found together along Commonwealth Avenue. This person was not of the same age, nor even of the same gender, as the previous lover who had so bitterly and yet blithely gutted my life, and while, as I say, this novelty struck in me both terror and surprise, it also altered me in ways I had not imagined possible. It was like discovering a new continent, both in this person—whose beauteous youth alone brightened the rooms, the avenues, the very landscape—and in myself. All of which is neither here nor there in the story of Ridley Wandor, seeing as Ridley Wandor's story is, fundamentally, the one I wish to tell; but I mention it simply to make clear that by the time of my inquiries, by the time I discovered what had happened—though not, yet, perhaps, at the time at which it happened—I was a completely, or at least substantially, different person from the one who had languished in old Eric's Kilburn flat, contemplating deaths both professional and personal.

In that sense, of course, the weight I felt in my time in that flat was neither imaginary nor misguided: it was killing me, it did kill me, that heavy, lonely, ultimately drear summer in London; only the death was of a Tibetan or a Tarot sort, the death that implies rebirth, a necessary darkness beyond which shines the light. It seemed like a suspension, a lifelessness without end; as if, for good or ill, I would never feel again. But by the time I dragged myself back across the Atlantic at August's end, to rejoin Copley and the rest of my too-familiar colleagues, I was already dimly aware of my snake's skin cracking, aware that the season had been—hibernant indeed—a time of invisible growth, the results of which must now be made manifest. So that when, in early October, I met my old acquaintance and new love—and it was, I must make this eminently clear, a case on both sides of love at first sight, although it took me the longer to recognize that flame, as I, for all my years, had never felt it before, and certainly would never have expected to feel it for a soul cloaked in that unexpected body, so thoroughly other from my former predilections—but anyway, by the time I met this inevitable love, I was *recognizable* to that person, in a way I perhaps wasn't yet then to myself, but certainly wouldn't have been to anyone at all several months before. In old Eric's sunlit flat, in that dark time, I had died and been reborn, and several short weeks later that new self was just taking form, its shape just becoming visible, in that small and overheated upstairs gallery at the far end of Newbury Street where my former colleague's—and my beloved's former professor's—paintings were on display. The room was uncomfortably crowded, the wine unpalatable and vinegary. Even the pictures themselves were ugly, great squiggling scratches of paint in incongruously genteel colors with which one would never concede to decorate a home—old rose, Wedgwood blue—a sort of abstract art for the unloved maiden aunt. But in my memory, there is a glow about the scene, a tenderness in those hideous artworks, and a Proustian perfume in the smell of musty heating pipes and sweat-soaked woolens. One's experience so colors the world.

Which is why it was strange, when I pursued my inquiries of Ridley Wandor, that the person she was and the story I had conjured for her—so intensely that I was certain it was fact—were the fruits of a psyche I no longer held to be my own. And yet, the Ridley Wandor invented by the miserable sod I had been was the only Ridley Wandor that I either knew or could imagine. Given what happened in fact, which did not coincide at all with what I had imagined, and which was considerably more tragic, it would seem that my invention was not, for all my errors, utterly incorrect; but by the time I knew the facts, it was as if I were heaving about a dead person invented by a dead person, and it was difficult to think of her life as anything but a story.

Which is why, you see, it must be told. Precisely in order to transcend its storyness, to make clear that this is not the invented story of a woman who existed only in my imagination, but the real story of a flesh-and-blood, breathing, sentient creature, someone far more real than I ever wanted or allowed her to be.

It has occurred to me that in those heavy summer months which in retrospect I seem, in spite of the sunlight, to have spent either in the library or in bed, Ridley Wandor thought she was reinventing herself. I, who was in fact being reinvented, thought only that I was dragging myself through time, towards death—in the sense, at the very least, that death was my study at the time; but also, I shamefully admit, far more literally than that—and if I considered invention it was indeed with regard to Ridley Wandor, whom I thought, still more in the wake of her tear-stained confessional, I was creating through my powers of psychological deduction, attributing to her syndromes and disorders with which I was only vaguely acquainted in order to explain to myself her ultimately understandable, and even rather ordinary, oddities. I was wrong. Of course. She may have been being created, or re-created, in that period, but not—in any but the most theoretical sense—by me. While I was changing without knowing it. Which would suggest that while I thought myself sensitive to the least fibrillation in that world, I in fact sensed very little at all. I can admit this now, because I am different from how I was then; and also, most importantly, because I am no longer alone. Because I don't hate everything, as I then hated Ridley Wandor and the unseen Wandor *mère* and dead Eric, once I knew of him, and the black dog in the neighbor's garden gnawing at its chain, and above all and most tediously, myself. (Of course I still sometimes have occasion to loathe, either myself or others or both; but a certain venom is gone, a certain fire. I am forced to wonder whether I have become a less interesting person as a result, or more specifically, a person less interesting to me. On some level, there is no doubt that this is true; but I am also aware of the argument that my late lack of interest in myself is actually a simply good thing.)

Ridley Wandor. I was there at the beginning of what would be the end, but I didn't know it, and couldn't see it, because I was too preoccupied with the story I was constructing for her, a story that seemed plausibly enough like the truth, at the time and to me. (Though perhaps only to me. After my first conversation with Copley about Ridley Wandor, I did not speak of her, nor of my theories about her, to anyone, so cannot know what force they might have carried.) In short, I was too busy playing God to notice, and as a result I acted like a dog.

After the tearful evening visitation, I did not see her for over a week, perhaps even a fortnight. Then I ran into her on the High Road, just as I got off the bus from Swiss Cottage, laden with groceries from the Waitrose. Her hands were free— those puffy appendages proved quite serviceable, in the event— and she offered to help me. Shell-suited again, she appeared more cheerful, with perhaps even a rosy dusting on her wan and suety cheek. Her lank hair was parted, combed, and her titter wantonly enthusiastic.

"Feeling better?" I offered, jauntily.

"You are, too, I see. Up and about to the shops."

"Indeed."

We proceeded past the recently installed blue council dumpster, which was covered with chalky, wavery drawings of knives and guns of various sizes and which announced in large, stenciled white letters on each side, BRENT COUNCIL WEAPONS AMNESTY.

"I'm sure it helps to be settled in with a new patient," I observed, wanting to show that I remembered our conversation. "How is the old fellow? And how do you find his daughter— you were concerned about her?"

Ridley Wandor's laugh revealed the points of her teeth. "Oh, time moves on, I'm afraid. Time moves on. The old gentleman passed. Very suddenly. I'd only been there three days."

"I *am* sorry." I was: while this eventuality only reinforced my strong sense of her illness, either psychotic or supernatural, I imagined it could do little to bolster her shaky self-confidence.

"It was a good thing, really"—she shifted the Waitrose bags from one hand to the other—"because I hadn't had time to think a mean thing about him. Really. He was a dear old fellow. Horribly frail, but nice, you know? So I realized it wasn't my fault. It couldn't have been."

"How cheering," I said. "But you didn't ever genuinely believe . . . ?"

"I don't know. I honestly don't. You know, on the second day, I put him back in his bed after lunch—he sat in a chair to eat his lunch, even on the day he died, very proper, like—anyway, I put him back into bed and I bent to raise the bars—you know, for these very old ones, who forget, you have to have the bars, or they fancy they can pop up and run off at any moment and they end up in a heap on the floor with a broken hip. So I'm reaching for the bars, and he cries out, 'Don't! Don't do it!'"

I opened the rusting gate with my foot: we had reached our common house.

"'Don't do what?' I say. 'You've got to lie still, Mr. Ober,' I say. And he has a look of absolute panic on his face, his mouth wide on all his teeth and his eyes popping"—Ridley Wandor dropped the plastic bags down on the front walk, raised her hands up beside her face, and imitated the old man's grimace: it was, at least on her visage, ghastly—"and he says, 'Don't put the dirt on!' 'What are you on about, Mr. Ober?' I ask him. 'There's no dirt here. We're all nice and clean.' And he says, 'I'm in my tomb and all alone. You've put me in my tomb and now you're going to cover me with dirt.' He started to cry. I tried to cheer him up, but he wasn't having it. 'Alone in my tomb. Please, no dirt!' he kept saying." She paused, and sighed.

"That's absolutely horrible," I said. "Horrible."

"Well, it made me feel better, actually—not right then, but later. The next day, when he died. Because I realized that he knew all along he was dying, see. He was just off by one day. And if he knew he was dying, then it wasn't anything to do with me. Nothing to do with me at all."

"Except," I could not refrain from suggesting, "that he was right, no?"

"How do you mean?"

"Well, you had come, essentially, to put him in his tomb, so he was right to be afraid of you."

Ridley Wandor considered this for a few moments, and set her chin. It jutted vastly as she made up her mind. "I don't think that's true. I really don't." She brushed at her shell-suit top, a mauve and fuchsia number I had seen only from a distance before—when she was in the garden with her rabbits and I at my spy's perch. I could see up close that it was both ragged and dirty: many threads had been pulled, doubtless by vicious little bunny claws, and there were discolorations of various sizes and hues dotted across her front. "The place I am now—a young man—he agrees with me. We talked about it."

"A young man? I thought you only cared for the elderly."

"He's the—well, the nephew, I suppose, of the gentleman, Mr. Fortyce. He calls him Uncle Howard. He seems to live there sometimes, but I don't think all of the time."

"I see." I bent to pick up the bags she had been carrying for me. "Thank you—" I started; but she spoke over me, with unaccustomed eagerness, and the pinkness in her cheek began to deepen and spread.

"I've got a photo—would you like to see?"

She pressed upon me a blurred Polaroid pulled from her mauve pocket: taken outdoors, in front of a red brick building, it showed Ridley Wandor, voluminous in the silky black shirt in which she had wept, grinning nervously beside a slight dark man of uncertain age—but then so, too, was she of indeterminate age—with a bushy beard and a wing of hair falling over his brow. He was younger than she, of that I felt certain. His nose looked sharp, but it was impossible to tell, just as it was impossible to tell whether behind his beard he was smiling. He had his arms crossed over his chest, and he leaned towards Ridley Wandor in the picture just as she leaned a little towards him, and the effect was rather playful—in a disturbing sort of way.

"How nice," I said.

"He's my friend—my new friend. We just talk and talk," she said. "You understand—you're my friend too—how important that is. Why, you practically saved my life the other day, bless you."

"It was nothing."

"I'd like a photo of us, too—of you and me. For my scrapbook. I like to have pictures of people so that when I talk about them to Mum she can see who I mean."

"How is your mother?"

"Better, thank you. Just fine. She was a bit discombobu-lated when Terrence called—"

"Terrence?"

"In the photo—the man—my new friend."

"I see."

"She doesn't much like it when people call. Confuses her. She'd rather I didn't go out, really."

"I see—Miss Wandor, I must—"

"But he's very persistent—" She said this almost with a squeak, insisting on the sybillant syllable: per-*sis*-tent. "I think—I don't mean to be vain, but I think he has something of a thing for me." She was quite red by now, and huffing and tittering. I found more than ever that I could not look at her. I had in hand all my plastic bags—eight or nine of them—and I could feel my ten fingers purpling from the trapped blood.

"How could he not, my dear? How could he not?" I real-ized, as I spoke, that I had adopted the diction and tones of Copley, and I felt I had a sudden insight into the extent to which he was a liar. I thought more about this fact—a fact about me as much as about Copley; about how long I had known him and how I had refused, for all I had on some level felt his falsity, to acknowledge it—anyway, I thought consider-ably more about this fact than I thought about Terrence.

Or rather: insofar as I thought about Terrence at all, I thought of him as a creation of Ridley Wandor's (just as she was, at that stage, only my creation to me). I did not believe in him. Not that I didn't believe the man existed, but that I did not believe in her relationship with him. The very photograph produced as proof of their tie only served to feed my skepticism: this might be a posed photo with a stranger at a bus stop, with a café waiter or a vagrant. And even if it was the photograph of the nephew of the ancient Ridley Wandor was then tending, what did that say or prove of the man in question, but that he was at least moderately polite and had acceded to her request for a deathside souvenir snap? She described him as her new friend; next to whom I—who barely knew the woman and could not bear her—apparently qualified as an old friend . . . and had she not said that she wanted a similar photograph of me for her files? For the doctored autobiography, that is, on which she fed her mother, and had doubtless fed her mother for years, so that Wandor *mère*, rather than fearing for the sanity of her misfit offspring, rather than ever suspecting the overgrown girl's murderous powers, instead could imagine her as amply friended as she was plump, cushioned upon all sides, through all her adult years, by the smiling men and women of remote acquaintance that she had chivvied into fantastical life at home. In short, I thought of Terrence only as Ridley Wandor's imaginary friend. I was both wrong, and somehow right. I was above all, it would seem, fatally inattentive.

I was attentive, instead, to other clues, clues that seemed to answer the questions I, the prosecutor, had formulated in Ridley Wandor's trial-inside-my-head. Yet another of her patients had died, more swiftly than any that had gone before. This in itself seemed worthy of note. I suspected that Fortyce in his turn would not be long for this world, and made a mental note to ask about him at our next encounter: I remembered the name. I memorized it, so that there would be no confusion, so that if she had moved on, and even on again—so that if her charges kept dying like flies—I might nevertheless keep track of them. I mistrusted her good cheer. I ascribed it not to Terrence—him I brushed from my thoughts like a midge—but rather to her successful continuation of, indeed her successful reconciliation to, her dastardly mission. I had seen, so I thought, in her earlier tears a stage of remorse, a regret; and now, not so long after, and but one death further on, I was seeing her beyond remorse, in some state of growing jubilation. And what, in all this, of the ultimate victim, the invisible Mrs. Wandor?

Her daughter claimed that the mother was feeling "better," but when had I known of her as unwell? (Aside, of course, from her putative inability to climb stairs, the reason, I was to believe, that I had never seen her.) If the mother had been unwell, then all those weeks before it had been the mother I was hearing through the bathroom pipes, in such distress. That woman had been not merely sick but weeping, too; and the taps had been turned on—surely not an old woman's instinct?—to mask the sound. Which meant that Ridley Wandor had been with her mother, had most certainly made her cry, had tried to hide the sound from any possible listeners (me and only me). It made sense, then, that she would curry favor in my quarter, would seek me out as she seemed so studiously to do: if she had heard my tread above that night, but even if she hadn't, she might suspect that I suspected her—of cruelty, of abuse, if not yet (and why not yet? who knew?) of the attempted murder of her mother. She had said that her mother wanted to see photographs of all of Ridley's friends; and yet she'd claimed that the older woman did not like her daughter to have callers: this was not logical. Clearly, I thought, this illogic bore the traces of invention: the sweet old woman, incapacitated howsoever she was, delighted in imagining her girl's life peopled. Who, then, would balk at the interruption of their solitude by attentions from outside? Surely it was Ridley who, even as she had built for her mother's fantasy (and her own) a life full of fictional Ridley-friends, had, with concomitant zeal, stripped her mother's invalid life of all outside society altogether. I cast my mind back over the weeks—by then as many as I had plastic bags in hand to cut my circulation—of my tenure in old Eric's flat: I had seen no guests come or go; had heard no alien steps on the walk, nor the muffled buzzer of their door. Not once. The old woman was trapped alone with the Hunters, those infernal thumping rabbits (whose cage-jangling I sometimes fancied I discerned, if I was in my sitting room late at night), and with her daughter. Four days a week with no human companionship at all—and three enveloped by the deceptively mercenary, whey-faced child. Mrs. Wandor, I mused, must be in terror of her daughter, to comply with the younger woman's wishes even when she was off "caring" for the elderly. Poor Mrs. Wandor. Poor prisoner. Poor murder-victim-to-be.

The degree to which their lives were sport for me—were a story with which I dabbled for my own diversion—was inadmissible to my supposedly moral self. Because in the same wholehearted but artificial way that one believes the horrors of True Crime—fact titillating in the manner of fiction—I really did believe that the daughter—so profoundly did she give me the creeps—was in danger of murdering the mother. And I did believe that she was guilty, in one way or another, of having hastened the deaths of several of her patients. I believed those things with a God-like certainty. But, cur that I was, I never had any intention, no intention whatsoever, of acting to avert disaster, let alone of seeking justice for the crimes I imagined committed. I have asked myself why this was so: did I not really believe in Ridley Wandor's guilt? Perhaps not wholly, but sufficiently. Insofar as I believed in Ridley Wandor, I believed her guilty. But in that summer so far from all that was familiar to me, in which I barely believed in my own flesh, which I could bite or pinch or draw blood from, in that summer of strange enclosedness, in which the vast panes of glass in my flat, through which I could observe so much about which I felt so little, seemed to travel with me outside into the city, like an invisible protective pope-mobile, I viewed the entire world at a muffled remove, without emotion. I was certain that Ridley Wandor planned to kill her mother, sooner or later, and obsessed with finding proofs to substantiate my theory. I was vaguely curious to see whether the death would occur before I left London or not, not least because part of me felt that such a death would provide a satisfying end to the story of my lustreless time there; while another part of me fretted because the death, were it to take place "in time" (hideous that I thought thus of it, but I did), might also seem the beginning, as much as the ending, of a story, one in which I feared I might take a still more lively interest. That is to say, I was anxious, even as I waited without qualms for the daughter to murder the mother, that the act would give me pause, make me want to stay on in that limbo state, in that limbo city, from which I quietly longed to escape.

And it was only in that way that the pair of them had any meaning at all.

Needless to say, there was no death in the flat below me in my time. Even Mr. Fortyce seemed, at first, blessed with atypical longevity. A further two weeks passed before my next, and penultimate, Wandor encounter, in the front hall this time, where I sorted through the circulars on the table in search of my mail, when the entrance to the ground-floor flat was opened. Ridley Wandor emerged stealthily—opening the door only part of the way, just far enough to slide herself sideways through it—but was unable to contain the powerful sawdusty, animal smell that emerged around her, and bespoke the proximity of the Hunters, a great seeping cloud of *eau de lapin*. She was less thoroughly delighted than usual to see me, almost embarrassed; and I could understand why. She was dressed up, more so than I had ever seen her, in a flowered blouse with a Peter Pan collar and a navy skirt, and sporting shoes which, although distorted by her broad feet, were an inexpensive but adequate version of an elegant pump. Not only were her hands perfectly manicured—their talons an unexpected and inescapable vermilion—but her very face was made up, shockingly, fully. She did not have a face that lent itself to maquillage, given that her only distinguished feature was the great chin; and the effect, thus, of the kohl and creams and shadows was, to my horrified eye, clownishly grotesque, as if her eyes had been smeared with soot and her lips with rust-flecked grease.

She tittered, nervously, vaguely; it was I who pinned her with questions.

"Don't you look lovely, my dear Miss Wandor! Where are you off to?"

"It's my day off."

"And noontime—a lunch engagement, perhaps?"

She blushed. The skin beneath her makeup took on its fiery glow, a hue incompatible with the artificial surface.

"Surely it's not old Mr. Fortyce you're lunching with?"

She whinnied, glanced coquettishly from the corner of her insipid eye.

"Is the old man still with us?"

"Oh yes." She seemed relieved. "He's been weak, but I think he's rallying. Terrence says that it's happened before, that—"

I had forgotten Terrence altogether. "Is he your date, then?"

"Who?" Again, the furtive eye roved, this time turning back to her flat.

"This Terrence fellow—you're lunching with him today?"

"Don't tell my mother. Please don't."

"Of course not, Miss Wandor." I waved my letters at her with mock severity. "How could I, when I've not had the pleasure of making the dear lady's acquaintance?"

"Please, no, please, shush," Ridley Wandor admonished frantically, blanching beneath the rouge and waving her hands. She sighed, then whispered, "It's a very thin door, really. Please don't do this to me. Please. She may be right there. Listening."

It was after this—after seeing, on Ridley Wandor's plain and painted face, a look of such genuine distress, of frank misery washed with—it was unmistakable—fear—it was then that I began to reconstruct and reconstrue. There was, beneath the bunny smell, the smell of fear upon her: I couldn't deny it, and had to take it into account.

Who, in the end, was whose prisoner? I was forced to ask myself. And what manner of woman, or of monster, might the old Wandor *mère* prove to be? It was the fear that shook me: it rendered Ridley Wandor's unfortunate physiognomy almost, flickeringly, loveable; it certainly had the undesired and complicating effect of rendering her fully human. The ungainly little-girl's blouse, the wavering of her burstingly plump feet in the straining pumps, the smear of rouge across her slab of cheek— these things which had seemed but a moment before the stuff of faintly unappetizing comedy were suddenly vivid and real in a thoroughly other way, were suddenly tufts of cotton batting in my throat, and my eyes were awater and my voice lost—lost to the true agony of Ridley Wandor's days, of the jaunty little displays against despair, the grins and circus colors, so futile and so very, very sad—and it was all I could do to mumble my excuses and retreat, letters to my chest, up the stairs.

I had preferred it the other way. Still, even in those last days in that Kilburn flat when, as I would subsequently discover, the greater part of my transformation was complete; when, indeed, one might assert that my pupal stage was nearing its close—still, even then, I felt my sorrows to be by far the greatest, my wounds the source of the only real blood. I did not want to see, let alone to believe in, the sorrows of others. And while now it seems to me evident that I was only able, at the last, to discern the great, glowing aura of grief around Ridley Wandor because I was, myself, nearly healed, yet at the time I took this illumination to be an affront. An assault. For which—who would not?—I blamed her.

This said, this instant, this glance, which forced me to reevaluate the life I had constructed for the Wandors—it rekindled my interest in the invisible mother. Tender of the rabbits. Supposedly invalid. But perhaps what kept her from coming to the door, from coming up the stairs, was her rage—a pure rage like ethyl alcohol, a blue flame of fury that turned upon her milky child whenever the aging girl came home. I did not need to ask whence that rage might come, nor at what it might be directed: I had experienced it myself, had been consumed, inflamed, indeed, by such rage and knew it for a force beyond reason. That rage, I knew, was pure passion, purer than any love or lust, than any hope. I could have summoned it there—who can't summon the devil if they try?—but preferred to imagine it into the flat below, into the unseen and untested heart of old Mrs. Wandor. Only such a force could explain the expression—and try as I might, I could not forget the expression—that had muddied Ridley Wandor's bland and hopeful face. The tears brought to me through the bathroom pipes took on new meaning, as did the constant efforts to befriend me, as though with each titter and unwelcome pat Ridley Wandor were in fact howling, like some possessed child in a horror film, "Help me. Save me. Free me from this hell."

This is not my story, not a story about me; but still I must interject that I had my reasons, even then—perhaps especially then—for not descending the stairs and rapping firmly on the Wandor door in order to lure the dragon from her lair. Chief among them was the knowledge that whether she was, in fact, an incandescent flame of searing fury, or an oppressed invalid tyrannized by her unstable daughter—and for all I knew she might be simultaneously both of those things and many more besides—whether one or the other, she would look exactly the same. She might be bulky and unkempt like her offspring, and toothless and bald in the bargain; or she might be neat as a pin, coiffed and even pretty, a tiny birdlike anomaly in the stinking rabbit mess. Whatever she was would reveal nothing, because to see her as any story I would tell would need to, I would have to see her through the eyes of her daughter. An impossibility. For as I well knew, if Copley had met Ridley Wandor, for example, he would not have seen what I saw, nor felt what I felt. And even that—what I saw, what I felt—was infinitely fungible.

I decided, then, a mere week before my departure, that my interest was prurient, that whatever stories about the Wandors, *mère et fille*, might have titillated my isolated imagination, and whatever stories might indeed be true—that I had no further interest in or truck with them. There were bills to be paid, loose ends to be tied, final notes to be hastily gathered from rare documents in the library—the stuff of distant but actual deaths suddenly again that much more real than the imaginary future deaths of my temporary neighbors: and so I banished Ridley Wandor—that expression! that costume!—from my thoughts. Fully. Altogether. In the beginning, when first she crossed my threshold, all I had wanted was that she *would not be*. And suddenly it became clear—a conjurer's trick of a different sort—that her ceasing to exist, her vanishing, was but a matter of my whim. Poof. Gone.

Be careful what you wish for. The moral of children's fairy tales is true. I didn't wish for the person who changed my life—I couldn't have, not in that guise. My life as it is now, benison and balm, is something I cannot wish even today to keep. I fear wishing as much as Ridley Wandor ever did. A tale of my child-hood recounted a little girl's visit to the Land of Lies. There, each lie she uttered was taken for the truth, each truth for a lie. This is not the perversity of an invented topsy-turvy realm: it is our very own, the land across which we trudge for the better part of our lives. And the same is true of our wishes, I have come to conclude: those held closest in our hearts—the wish for love, for our own success, my wish to escape from the small-town life and the oblivion of my minor institution—all these things are to be denied us, the truths the world will only scoff at. Ridley Wandor wished for love, and now I'm certain of it, for a release from the *huis clos* of her mother's flat (call it theirs if you will, but that smelly den was her mother's, first and fore-most), and for hope, for the hope of transformation. I had re-linquished that hope in my own life by the end of that summer, had cauterized, or thought to have cauterized, all shoots of op-timism in my inky abysmal cerebellum. And yet, as fate would show, it was only by ceasing to wish for the good that I was vis-ited by it.

And all the while, the dark wishes, fleeting, unfelt—Ridley Wandor was right. These are the wishes that bear fruit in spite of us. She wished her patients dead—but only in an exhausted instant—and they alarmingly obliged. I wished that Ridley Wandor would not be, and this, too, came to pass. Did I bring about her end? A court of law could only find me innocent— and yet?

I saw her only once more, on the day of my departure. I had hauled my cases into the weedy front garden to await the black cab ordered by telephone. (I had no interest, on this last journey out of my estival hell, in saving money by taking, instead, an exotically perfumed and uncomfortable minicab of the kind I had foisted on Copley.) It had occurred to me to say goodbye, on this last day to knock at last, for the first time, upon the Wandor door—but I had opted against. I owed her nothing; wanted only to purge my imagination of her sorry little life. I had, I told myself, too much to worry about, to consider the feelings of a woman, an imposition, that I barely knew. But she found me on the front walk, her little eyes popping at the sight of my luggage, her chin (surely not?) atremble. She must have been peering through the net curtain of her grimy bow window.

"You can't be? You're *leaving*? But I had no idea!"

"But a summer's retreat, Miss Wandor. Duty calls, alas. You have your patients, I have my students."

"A photo?" she bleated. "You must let me have a photo!"

I could not refuse. She disappeared into the house even as my eye was on my watch, secretly cursing the tardy taxi and wondering whether I would have to go back upstairs to call the company again. (Surely, I groused inwardly, surely promptness and efficiency were what one paid extra for? But perhaps it was merely for the lacquer-black vehicle and its ticking meter?)

We were to be frozen in Polaroid. Together. A passerby—one of the frequently shirtless youths from the council block opposite, a boy I recognized—was enlisted to do the dirty work.

"Please, take two!" exhorted Ridley Wandor, with frantic good cheer. "We'll be an ocean apart, and that way we can each have one."

The boy, saturnine, complied; and while I thought he might make off with the camera afterwards, he clearly found it beneath his notice. He did not smile or frown, and muttered only a sullen "Cheers" as he moved on.

This had taken a good five minutes, and still there was no sign of my taxi. Ridley Wandor strove to make conversation as the pictures emerged, our outlines looming slowly with the black maw of the front door behind us. "Did you get all your work done?" she asked, and "Has it been a pleasant stay for you?" And "What will you remember most about London, then?" to which I answered, without irony, "You, Miss Wandor. Of course it will be you." This provoked the most vivid blushing and a renewed trembling of the chin.

In return, I asked about her mother, who was, as ever, "better, thank you"; and I asked about Mr. Fortyce who, I was told, had "passed, very suddenly, last week. A terrible blow for Terrence, you know."

"What of your work?" I asked.

"I start a new lady on Monday," she said. "She's in slightly better health, I'm told, which I'm glad of."

I nodded, my eyes on my watch.

"But Terrence and me," she blurted, "that's still going." She laughed, and glanced at me sidelong, smirking. "I can't believe it, some days. I think I'm dreaming." Her face was red, and her eyes were shining with almost-tears.

"That's very nice," I offered, charitably. "I'm happy for you."

"They're ready now—one each." She gave the snapshots a final shake, one in each hand, like tiny wings in the afternoon air.

And then there we were, immortalized together, she in the mauve and fuchsia shell suit, a blur of color, her tiny eyes slitted against the sun and her lank hair, which was—I do remember—very greasy, glistening. She stands very close to me, her pink brushing my navy jacket. I am the same height as she, but slight, and dark, and darkly clad, and my arms are crossed over my chest—as Terrence's arms were, in his photo—and the pull at my lips is a grimace, or a wince. The two photos were almost identical; I slipped the one she proffered into my jacket pocket and, by then desperate, explained that I was awaiting my cab and must call to check on it.

"I'll do it," she said, and rushed in.

And then the taxi appeared, at once, as if he had been waiting at the corner for her to vanish; and he—a burly older fellow, a drinker, with greenish sweat-stains on his pale blue shirt—dismounted, grabbed the larger case while I lugged the other, and bundled them and me into his chariot and away.

At the airport, as requested by the real estate agent—by the spotted Sheila Cooke—I put the keys to my voyeur's hideaway into a padded envelope and into the post before boarding the plane, and in so doing shut out all memories—of the sun-filled sitting room, of the gardens below and windows full of life opposite, of old Eric's fond kitchen table, of the Wandors, of the High Road, of the terrible weight of my limbs in those everlasting months—I shut them all away for a long time to come. I welcomed the enclosed, biscuity smell of the jumbo as if it were pure oxygen, and thrilled at the prospect of my little plasticized meal: between two destinations, anything is possible. No wishing, no hope, just the pure thrill of *maybe*. I never saw Ridley Wandor again. For a long time, I did not give her another thought.

And yet. And yet I had not been lying when I said that I would remember her above all else. When, taking the jacket to the cleaners several months later—it felt like years, my life was by then so very altered—I came across the Polaroid, I saved it to show to my still newly beloved, who heard, then, in parodically dirgelike terms, about the summer preceding our meeting. Finally, in my new, shared home in the brownstone on Commonwealth Avenue, with the first snow falling outside and a solemn white light seeping into the room, with my beloved's legs across mine as we sat on the sofa (who, ever, could have envisaged me in such posture, with such a person? not I, who could not even have wished for it), it was there, though still laughing less than kindly at the hideous shell suit, the grease-glinted hair, at the drab house behind and its straggling weeds about our feet (how ever had I found it charming, even on the first day, when poverty and entrapment so powerfully hung about it like a vapor?), it was seeing us there, her ebullience; my barely veiled distaste, for which I felt a pang of genuine remorse—it was only then, at last, that I was able to wish her well.

By then, had I but known it, I was too late. Which I would discover when, at Easter time, I was to take my beloved, so much younger than I, for an extravagant week in London, which I purported to know the more intimately, although what, in reality, did I know? We stayed in Soho, at the ruinous but thoroughly charming Hazlitt's, surrounded nightly, even in the chill spring, by the sprawling street revelries of youth, of my beloved's generation in their glory. Copley, when I told him of it, claimed himself proud of me; and in truth, I harbored a clandestine, even exultant, pride of my own.

The pilgrimage, hand in hand, to the burial place of my former self, was not my choice, but once mooted, seemed essential. It was not my idea, either, to ring the Wandors' bell, but that, too, seemed of significance, a final laying to rest of all I had thought to know, had wildly—insanely, I knew by then—imagined about the innocent, rather pathetic, mother and daughter.

But it was a young Spanish woman in her late twenties who came to the door, slender and hook-nosed with a sleek chignon and stylish clothes, a cigarette in hand. She had moved into the flat two months before, she said; it was newly renovated, we were welcome to see, with colorful kilims and Japanese-style blinds, all-new appliances and a fresh coat of paint. The garden was well tended, too, and seemed to be of long standing, she said, for which she was grateful to her predecessors; but she knew nothing about them. Nothing at all. Perhaps Mr. Taha—

his name, long forgotten, brought with it a whiff of rabbit, of Ridley Wandor's personal fragrance—might know where they had gone? Or the couple next door—Lynch, that was it—who seemed to have been part of the neighborhood for years.

Curious though I was to see the flat, to ask the woman if she, like me upstairs before her, had been duped into imagining that people had been happy there—I merely thanked her, and offered good wishes, and that would have been an end to it. As we retreated, the front walk, on which Ridley Wandor and I had been photographed not so long before, seemed a completely other place, overlaid with a semblance . . . of what? of gentility? hope, even? that it had not known before.

"Oh well," I said, as I pulled the still-rusty, still-squeaky gate shut behind us. "It's a shame. And rather strange—after all, they'd lived there for years. They were sitting tenants. She explained it to me at tedious length."

"We should ask the neighbors," insisted my dear one, oddly eager. "It's such an anticlimax, otherwise. I wanted to *see* her, after the photo and everything."

"Probably the old woman died, at last, and Ridley Wandor set off on her new life. I'm glad, really."

And I was: I didn't need to know more. But I wasn't alone. "I'll ask if you won't," came the sweet voice, already halfway up the Lynches' walk. "You'll be glad we did. You've got to learn to say yes a little more, you know. It's part of my job to teach you."

Mrs. Lynch was Irish, her creampuff physique and bluish cloud of hair familiar, though whether I had actually noticed her the previous summer or merely saw in her the template that haunted the Kilburn High Road and comprised the queue in the malodorous local post office I couldn't say. Her voice was high, and lilting, and when I mentioned the Wandors she took my forearm with a clawlike grip, unexpected given the plumpness of her hand, and insisted that we come in for tea.

"You were a friend of Ridley's, weren't you? Upstairs, last summer. She spoke very highly of you: a blessing, it was, she said, to form a friendship in your own house. She was a lonely girl—oh, hardly a girl, I know, but I'd practically seen her grow up, hadn't I, so she always seemed a girl to me. A troubled girl, too. So sad."

"And what was sad?" my beloved asked. "Did her mother die, then?"

"Oh no. She's a tough old nut, Betty—a strange woman, and I always wondered if she tippled, but she's a tough old nut."

"So why did they move? After all these years?"

"You don't know about it then."

"About what?"

"*They* didn't, did they?" She fixed her eye upon me, all but accusing. "It was terrible. A tragedy. Sit. The kettle's just boiled. Sit."

And so, in the rosy chintz parlor of Margaret Lynch, we heard the story of the Wandors, *mère et fille*, and of Ridley's sad end.

There had been a father, but that was before Kilburn—in South London, somewhere. And there'd been a brother, the story went, a younger brother and the apple of their mother's eye. And an accident—bicycling, the two children, near the railway tracks—and then no brother anymore. The story was (as of course it must be, although who would ever know whether it was true?) that the mother never forgave the daughter, and that the daughter never forgave herself. Certainly Ridley then never left her mother, and although she was a young woman, or youngish, when they moved into the flat, and although her mother then was far from old, their rhythms and manners and routines were those of the elderly. Betty was reclusive, pinched; her daughter friendly enough, but always distant.

And the rabbits: that mania—there were so many of the creatures—had caused some distress among the neighbors, and more than one complaint, not least from Margaret Lynch herself, whose attempts at a vegetable garden were repeatedly and summarily devoured. The rabbits: nobody knew whether they were Ridley's or Betty's choice—each had claimed to Margaret that they were the other's pride and joy, and could not therefore be sacrificed. For years, they kept those rabbits, breeding them, dressing them up in little costumes, photographing them, doting on them as if they were their children, the only thing they loved and shared. Because of the bad blood over the rabbits, Margaret Lynch explained, nobody in the road had been especially friendly with the Wandors. Civil, to be sure, but not more than that. Not least, she whispered, because of the smell—had I not smelled it? she asked, because old Eric had complained of it in his day, said the front hall stank, sometimes, and even Margaret, sitting in her garden, had occasionally been enveloped by it in waves. It drove her dog—that damned black dog on its chain, which I only then remembered—quite mad. Although that, she insisted, was neither here nor there, in the end.

Betty had always had bad hips, and the preceding September—not long after my departure—the NHS had scheduled her, at last, for the double replacement. Her daughter took her to the hospital, and visited her there; but then, with Ridley's work schedule—four days on, three off, I knew it well—was unable to come for a spell. When, eventually, she should have come, she didn't; and then it was discovered that she hadn't been at work at all; and when Social Services finally came by the house (it took them a week or more; but they couldn't bring the old woman home without Ridley there to care for her, so someone did come, in search of her) there were only the rabbits, and they, all but one, were dead in the hutches, and the stench unbearable. The last rabbit was euthanized, Margaret Lynch informed us solemnly, by the RSPCA, who deemed it best; and there wasn't a soul in the road who was sorry.

"Where had she gone?" asked my beloved, goggle-eyed, full of the story that was nothing, to those dear ears, but story, as its protagonists were made only of words, not flesh. "Had she run away?"

"That's what everyone thought, at first," said Margaret Lynch, nibbling daintily, almost vindictively, at a Peak Frean's bourbon creme, so that I could tell the story was no more than that to her either; and was it—for I, too, was agog—any different for me?

It was weeks, maybe it was months—it was dark and blustery, Margaret Lynch remembered the day: it was late November—before they found her body. Fully clothed, in a ditch at the foot of a bluff in the Lake District.

"The Lake District?" I echoed, my first words for a very

long time; thinking, too, of the afternoon in our Boston apartment, November also, when we had laughed over the Polaroid.

"Near Grasmere. Indeed. A hardy American couple, out walking in spite of the weather—much was made of the weather. They found her. In her pink shell suit, poor love. That's what caught their eyes."

"Mauve and fuchsia," I said.

"Beg your pardon?"

"It was mauve and fuchsia."

Margaret Lynch raised an eyebrow, and nibbled some more. Like a rabbit.

"What happened?" asked my beloved, hands on knees, alert as a hound. "Was it murder? Was it suicide?"

"Well," said Margaret Lynch, with a twitch of the lips that looked very much like a smirk to me, "didn't everyone want to know?"

"And?" I saw the Ridley Wandor of my Polaroid, squinting, grinning, pale and awful: surely somebody had cared enough to find out?

"It proved difficult to say."

"Why's that?"

"Her neck had been broken." That fleshy padded neck, whose ringed deposits surfaced unbidden in my mind's eye, with such unnerving clarity, as if she lived there still, as if she were walking and breathing and tittering inside my head.

"It was a long time after, you know. She was quite . . . quite decomposed." She hesitated over the word, lips pursed. "They said," she went on, "that she could have fallen, or that she could have been pushed."

"But someone had seen her, up there? They must have—how did she get there? Who was she with?"

"Well, this is the strange thing: nobody had seen her. No one at all, except a tea-shop lady claimed to have served a woman who looked rather like her, in a shell suit that might have been that one. But it was still the high season then, wasn't it, back in September, and already a long time previously, and she said she thought that woman had had children in tow, which didn't make any sense at all, so the police couldn't take her too seriously."

"And so? And then?"

"They figured she didn't take the train up, because she would've been spotted. She's not the sort you'd necessarily remember, she wasn't special to look at—as you know—but she would've sat next to someone. She would've taken a taxi. Something."

"So she was driven."

Margaret Lynch shrugged, and nibbled.

"Terrence," I said.

"I beg your pardon?"

"Terrence. It must have been Terrence. Her boyfriend, or so she said."

"Boyfriend? Ridley?"

"Didn't she tell you about him?"

"It's the first I've heard of a boyfriend. And I read all the papers, I read everything they printed."

"He was the nephew—the nephew, I'm sure of it, of that fellow—what was his name? Fort? Fortnum? Fortyce. It was Fortyce, with a 'y.' The nephew."

"I remember *his* name, because one of the articles listed all her patients, the last six months of them, and nobody seemed to have noticed, but they were dying like flies all that time, one after another—shocking, really—and then someone suggested that she might, you know, that she might have had a problem, that she might have been doing them in, and that then, overcome with remorse, you know, she'd killed herself . . ."

"Does that seem likely?" I asked.

"Well, you knew her best," observed Margaret Lynch, with a narrowed eye. "When you think of it, with her mother, the burden of her mother, and their relationship really was very strange. And so private, nobody knows what was between them, and sometimes people snap, and . . ."

"This is pure speculation, surely, Mrs. Lynch. Is it not?"

"But isn't it all, don't you know?" She moved to her bookshelf, by the window, and withdrew a cheap plastic album—doubtless bought in one of the tatty shops on the High Road, forever associated in my mind with Ridley Wandor—from atop the Encyclopaedia Britannica. I could hear the black dog barking out the window. "Fortyce," she said, "Fortyce. I've kept all the clippings." She rifled through the pages, peering in the weak sunlight, and paused to retrieve her glasses from the pearly string around her neck. I watched her looking, her downy bosom rising and falling, her blue eyes intent behind their glasses, the common greed of her search, her desire to own the story in all its melodrama, as if some reflected glory or infamy might fall upon her: God-like, doglike. So unlike me, yet the same.

"Here it is—" Her finger, clawlike, arthritic I noticed now, upon the yellowing newsprint page in its plastic casing. "Fortyce.

Eighty-two, like many of the others, entirely alone. No living relatives at all. It says so, right here."

I walked to the window, leaned over her shoulder, followed with my own eye the beady lines of type. She smelled of scented soap, an old-lady smell, but a clean one. The dog continued to bark. That was indeed what it said: old Fortyce had been alone in the world. Not a single living relative. Cremated by the state.

"There was a man named Terrence. A younger man. She met him through Fortyce, whether they were actually related or not." I was raising my voice. "I know because I saw a picture of him, of the two of them together—he had a beard. He was small, and dark. And she was very odd, speaking about him, she'd get all breathy and coy, she didn't want her mother to know the nature of their—you realize—her awkwardness seemed very genuine."

"She was a very awkward girl," said Mrs. Lynch, blinking calmly behind her glasses. "If there were a young man, don't you think the police would've found him?"

"Not if they weren't looking," I said. "Not if nobody knew about him, if she didn't want people to know. I saw the photograph—"

"But you—" My beloved didn't want to cross me—I could detect the hesitation—but felt obliged. "But you have a photo of *the two of you* together. You said she insisted, because she thought you were such good friends—"

"That was different."

"How so?"

How so, indeed. I had myself thought Terrence a figment,

her imaginary friend. I had thought him a man conjured, like a ghost, onto the celluloid by the very force of her desire, willed into life as her patients were willed into death. And why would I think, now, that I had been in error before? Why, suddenly, should Terrence grow genuine limbs, with powerful—or not so powerful, but certainly lethal—muscles, animated by an unknowable malice? Why should he become not merely a real man, which I had never thought him to be, but a real man with a perverse desire to kill Ridley Wandor, than whom there was no more unfortunate innocent in all of Northwest London? And yet.

"She was odd when she spoke about him. She couldn't believe her good fortune. To be honest, I couldn't either. He was younger, he looked quite plausible in the photograph, and of course she, she—"

"Wasn't," said my beloved for me, "wasn't plausible."

"Certainly she wasn't lovely, nor young, nor well set up, nor always very clean—and it struck me as strange that a man, any man, whatever manner of man he might be, would see in her—"

"And you thought she'd made him up. Or at least, made up her relationship with him. You said so, to me. The way she embroidered and elaborated her relationship with you."

"She did tell me you were very good friends," said Margaret Lynch, clasping the album to her chest. "Is it not true? Were you not good friends?" Her eyes widened, and she dropped her glasses back on their string, letting them bump against her bosom. "And she didn't tell me about this Terrence fellow at all."

"I suppose, Mrs. Lynch, that it would depend upon your understanding of the word." I sighed. "It would be true to say that I had no better friend in London last summer; but that, in itself, doesn't say very much. I didn't know another soul."

"Were you friends or weren't you?" Mrs. Lynch was in earnest.

"Not especially, no. We were, I would say, friendly acquaintances. Yes. Friendly acquaintances describes it right."

"But she said you were very dear friends. To me, she said so."

"So it would seem."

"So if she told you and only you about this Terrence guy," interjected my beloved, "the question is, did she do it because she thought of you as her closest friend and the only one she could truly confide in; or did she do it because she thought that with you, who were leaving at the end of the summer and had no connection at all to anyone else in her life, she could make up any story she wanted, and somehow, somehow, just by telling it to you, make it more real?"

"I don't know," I said, aware that we had become a strain upon Margaret Lynch's hospitality, with my revelation that I was not Ridley Wandor's bosom companion. We had become a blot, or pair of blots, upon her rose chintz upholstery. And yet, for all my awareness, I was unable to stop, because I felt—wrongly, too late, and in sorry truth, only fleetingly—that a life was at stake.

"I didn't believe in Terrence then," I said. "But I think I may have been wrong. I think, perhaps, a deranged younger man—I think he could have—"

"It's all pure speculation, isn't it?" asked Mrs. Lynch, who had returned the album to its place atop the encyclopedia and was standing, arms open, as if to herd us out. "A very sorry tale."

"Perhaps I should tell the police."

"Tell them what?" asked Mrs. Lynch.

"I saw a photograph."

"It was ruled an accidental death," she said. "After everything was examined. There were no signs of struggle. And it's impossible to know if she jumped. She had reasons enough, even if she never laid a finger on those dead patients. Reasons enough."

"Where's her mother?"

"Betty Wandor's in a home, now, up Cricklewood way. It was the only solution, really. I haven't been to see her," said Margaret Lynch with a renewed pursing of her lips. "Because we were never really friendly. It would seem"—she made a sucking noise in her teeth—"artificial. The link, such as it was, was to the girl."

"Indeed."

I wondered again, later, about the mother, about Betty Wandor as she was known by her daughter, Ridley. Fearsome, controlling, perhaps even evil. But how kaleidoscopically different our visions are, and how far from reality might Ridley Wandor's picture of the world have strayed. I had been certain there was no Terrence, or at least, not that there was no man by that name, necessarily, but that whatever tangential connection he actually had to Ridley Wandor, it bore no resemblance whatsoever to the shining knight of her imagination. And yet now I felt certain, too, that there had been a man, who had at the least feigned an interest, had preyed upon the vulnerable, had murdered poor Ridley for reasons known only to himself. Granted, it did not, on the face of it, seem likely; but I was at a loss for likelihoods.

And yet, it occurred to me even as I spun this story—as I pictured the car, a dented blue Vauxhall, perhaps, in which Terrence, dark-haired, dark-jacketed, would have scooped up the exhilarated Ridley for their romantic escape (her first! surely in all her life, her first!) to the Lake District—a weekend in the country. I could see it, the crafty leer behind his beard, the flush across her pallid cheek, the fumbling of her eerily well-manicured hands; I could hear the buzzing late fly trapped inside their windshield, the fly he so expertly, and to her surprise, squashed beneath his thumb... Even as I spun this story, I could see that it was done to assuage my own guilt. All I had wished, and wished, and wished, was that she *would not be*. That she would simply vanish. And she had. Poof. Gone.

I feared the power of my will. Better that it be the force of Terrence's, whoever he might be. Who cannot summon the devil if they try?

And indeed, how long could her fate preoccupy me? It was past. The person I had been, the one who had known and loathed her, who had obsessed about her comings and goings, was as dead as she was. I was a new individual, newly loving and newly beloved, with a new future, and even a new London, spread like a feast before me. I didn't any longer sit behind glass and observe and invent; I had discarded my inventions. And what was

Ridley Wandor, after all, but the idle mind's invention of a bleak and lonely summer, a summer that in itself had all but ceased to exist? Were it not for the copious notes I had taken—on death; of course, on death—I might have believed that I had invented the entire season. Including the Polaroid. Which I subsequently, without ever speaking of it again, threw away.

On that, our last night in London, my dearest and I dined at the Ivy, that pricey frivolity capping a week of extravagance, more ruinous still and no less charming than the hotel. We observed women who looked like actresses and men who looked like politicians and we spoke about all the excitements and pleasures of the city as we had discovered it together, a city of verdant parks and crowded cafés, of the bustling claustrophobic stink of the Tube and the domed halls of Selfridges, of the endless spring flowers burgeoning in the still brisk air, of joy and possibility. Neither of us mentioned Margaret Lynch or Betty or Ridley Wandor, or the mysterious Terrence, indeed, which on that evening seemed only passingly strange; but we have never mentioned them since, which seems stranger still. And now, I believe, we never shall, because it is all but a story to us— was it ever anything but a story to me?—and one not ripe for retelling because its ending cannot satisfy. Because I'm guilty.

Does Terrence, I sometimes wonder, still have his copy of their Polaroid snapshot, his picture of Ridley Wandor grinning and leaning, alight at his side? I rather hope so, for her sake.